SALTWATER PRISON

Set far in the future, when mankind owes its survival to a vast network of ocean farms, CITY UN-
DER THE SEA tells the shattering story of a man
doomed to mindless serfdom in a colony of underwater slaves. Commander Jeremy Dodge knows he
must escape—yet in a twilight world filled with
savage, armed overseers and squadrons of man-
controlled killer fish, escape seems impossible. But
Jeremy Dodge is a man driven to fight—for the
only alternative is living death.

CITY UNDER THE SEA is more than a spellbinding
futuristic novel of adventure and survival. Kenneth
Bulmer's classic novel was the first to incorporate
the idea of undersea farming—and its chilling im-
plications in a world desperate for alternative food
sources—into the realm of science fiction. CITY
UNDER THE SEA stands at the forefront of Bulmer's
work—a prophetic, exciting novel.

D1570916

CITY UNDER THE SEA

KENNETH BULMER

AVON
PUBLISHERS OF BARD, CAMELOT AND DISCUS BOOKS

AVON BOOKS
A division of
The Hearst Corporation
959 Eighth Avenue
New York, New York 10019

First Equinox Printing, November, 1975
First Avon Printing, January, 1980

PROLOGUE

The water was deep and black and cold. Caught in the grip of crushing pressure, the water scarcely moved above the pelagic ooze, its profundity embalming reason, its bulk covering a vast gloom, drowning a mysterious world of eternal night.

The water thrust at the ooze of the ocean floor and thrust against the bleak wall of the escarpment, rising in barren, fissured, soaring columns of rock. Mudfalls draped rocky clefts like curtains and spilled out in undulating fans.

There was no color here—only the everlasting blackness.

Fissured and indented, the slopes of the scarp rose upwards in an unbroken, uninterrupted ascent, the longest continuous slopes in the world. Raking upwards at an ever steepening incline from the ocean floor, twenty thousand feet of lightless, plantless, virgin rock and mud supported and buttressed the continental shelf. Blackness unrelieved —and yet, lights. Lights everywhere. Luminous motes of color gliding and darting, poised, halting for a startled fragment of time, and then fleeing and disappearing, swooping and glowing in fierce, brainless hunger-satisfied triumph.

But now another source of light probed the depth. The bruised tag-end of the spectrum imperceptibly created an encompassing blueness, and as the mass of water above thinned, the blueness grew, lightening through the spectrum, pearling into a translucent twilight where the myriad lights from below flickered and faded with a spectral glimmer.

The bluffs of the continental shelf puffed out their bulging chests into the waters, shouldering from blackness into opaline radiance; but they themselves were drowned beneath a skin of water—a film of moisture negligible by comparison with the unplumbed depths below—but a film with merciless fingers of constricting pressure.

Under that pressure, strung along the very edge of the shelf, a chain of softly glowing pearls gleamed with a steady radiance. Each dome sent out its welcome beams of light, visible reminders, in that cruel undersea world, of comfort and warmth and rest. In the watery invisible atmosphere, the domes glowed like a diadem of stars.

There is movement around the domes. Shining forms, sparkling and glittering scales in the light, streamlined bodies, waving, glinting fins—fish. Fish by the billion. Schools of fish, colleges of fish, whole universities, twisting and turning—and yet—moving with strangely ordered purpose. With all their swarming to and fro, their playful scurryings, their gobbling for food, their sudden inexplicable surges, they never stray beyond the limits of the shelf, never seek to explore the blue depths beneath. And above them as the water pales ever greener and mellower and begins subtly to move in answer to other forces than those low agonized creepings of drowned currents, there are more fish, civilizations of fish both large and small, all responding in some mysterious way to an overriding controlling force.

Set forward on a jutting cliff that stands out like some sentinel finger from the undersea shelf, there hovers over rock and ooze only darkness—where surely there should be another link of light ringing the edge of the scarp. Fragmentary shadows flicker in the water. Lonely lights curve sharply, veer away. Into the twilight dimension seeps a murky cloud. A rolling cloud that is out of keeping with the crystalline liquid atmosphere. Sounds shatter the silence of the depths. Mutterings and flutings, the involuntary whistles of fish and the sharp, hard pinging of sonic waves. Shining bubbles rise and burst. The dome is silent and dead. Shapes clash and struggle around it. Giant jaws open wide.

Puny figures struggle—figures un-fishlike in this world of pitiless ferocity and unknowing cruelty—figures with four spindly inefficient appendages in place of powerful stream-lined fins and tail.

Tiny figures that have no place in this undersea world of darkness and cold and death.

CHAPTER ONE

The spaceport was crowded. The monorail was crowded. The streets bulged. Flyovers creaked under pressing humanity. It took him ten minutes before he could dial a taxi. The hotel lobby was crowded. The lift was crowded.

There were just too many damned people.

That was the trouble with Earth, of course. Nothing new in the thought. But coming back after ten years in space, it sort of hit him in the eye.

With just one person sitting waiting demurely by the window, the way he was feeling even his hotel room was crowded.

She wasn't the type to be overlooked. She attracted a crowd, she crowded your attentions and she more than crowded the shocking-pink orlon tube sweater. She stood up gracefully, with the fluid motion that, under the full effects of one whole gravity, he was still finding difficult, and turned to face him, smiling.

"Commander Jeremy Dodge?" Her voice was pleasant and smooth, and yet, in his frame of mind, still linked embarrassingly with the strident hum of the city.

"That's right." He waited for her to go on.

She made a little gesture with her left hand, the square cut nails gleaming. "I'm Elise Tarrant. Mr. Grosvenor's private secretary." She said it as though it explained everything.

Dodge said: "This Grosvenor. When do I meet him?"

He put his grip on the end of the bed. "He drags me off furlough—and believe me, Miss Tarrant, anyone who can persuade me to give up a mountaineering holiday on the Moon is a grade A persuader—and cajoles me down to Earth. I'm in rather a hurry. If you'd . . ."

"That is why I am here, Commander."

She was coolly amused, Dodge saw, and that made him feel uncomfortably small-boyish, which made him annoyed. It looked as though this self-possessed young lady had the power to shatter his composure. He drew his eyebrows down.

"Mr. Grosvenor asked me particularly to apologize for your holiday, but he feels that what he has to tell you will more than compensate." She paused, and then, with an air of gravity that caught Dodge's full attention, said: "It's such a big thing, really big, I mean, that your whole life will be altered."

Dodge grunted. "They told me that when we went on the first Jovian expedition."

She made a little moue of disgust. "So many billions that even the U.N. Treasury hasn't told the full story yet, and for half a dozen little balls of eternally frozen mud."

"You don't think much of the Space Force?"

"I think you're all heroes, sure. But I think you get too much applause and too much money and too many medals."

"Well, it's nice to know."

She caught her upper lip between her teeth. Dodge noticed how red the lips, how white the teeth. That pleased him, in an obscure way. The vero-colored makeup, flaunted by women he had seen on his brief journey from the spaceport to the hotel, had sickened rather than attracted him. The pace of the modern world was so hectic, that even ten tiny years could witness changes of astounding magnitude. She released the lip with a gesture of decision.

"I'm sorry, Commander. Perhaps I shouldn't have said that." She looked at him. "You'll have a better idea of how I feel when you've talked to Mr. Grosvenor and seen around . . ." She stopped speaking with such force that for a moment to Dodge it was like falling over a precipice of sound. Then she went on, but that quiet voice was uneven now, struggling to hold down some strong emotion. "If you are ready, Commander, we can start now."

"Start?" Dodge said, really wondering about that strange change of subject, that sharp cutting off of what the girl had been saying. "Start—where to?"

"To see Mr. Grosvenor. He is staying at the Blue Deep Hotel. It'll take us about an hour."

"An hour!" Dodge looked surprised. "Where is this Hotel, then, on the other side of the planet?"

Then, thinking of the traffic and the crowds he said sourly: "Or is it in the next block?"

She smiled. It was a sunrise in the spartan hotel room. Dodge began to see different angles to this enigmatic girl. He picked up his bag philosophically, prepared to play out this wild-goose chase until he could hear the straight talk from the lips of the persuasive Grosvenor himself.

The telephone rang.

Dodge answered. "Yes, this is Commander Dodge speaking. Who is . . ."

On the line there was a definite click as the receiver was replaced. Whoever had rung had merely confirmed that he was in his room, and had then rung off. Odd.

Elise Tarrant was staring at him uncertainly. He laughed shortly, and said: "Wrong number, I expect," and realized with a distinct sense of shock that he didn't think anything of the sort. And, what was odder still, he knew with a curious certainty that the girl didn't think so, either, and she knew that he knew she felt that. Elise crinkled up her nose, refusing to comment further, and Dodge picked up his bag and they left the room together. The electronic lock hummed cheerfully to itself as the door closed.

Dodge was happy to escape into the hissing maw of the Underground; at least there the atmosphere was air-conditioned and breathable. They hadn't got round to air-conditioning the streets yet, between the web-work of flyovers and vertical window-pierced cliffs, and the air there just wasn't breathable; not by the standards of a spaceman who lived off canned air and algae-produced oxygen all his life.

The idea of algae tanks for city-wide air-conditioning, suspended from every cross-over, attracted him fleetingly; it was the sort of whacky idea the Dodges could be relied on to dream up in any idle moment. The coast-hugging network of undersea farms would do well out of it, producing algae on an even greater scale than they now did for food-processing and the Space Force's uses. His Uncle Arthur had gone in for that aquiculture racket, the last he'd heard of him, and, oddly, it was about Uncle Arthur that this Grosvenor fellow wanted to talk. Be just like the old villain to have made his pile ploughing up the sea-bottom and herding fish and milking—well, they hadn't yet arranged to milk fishes; against nature or something. And, anyway, all these undersea ventures, the mile-deep oil wells and coal mines, the intense cultivation of sea-weeds and adapted marine plants, the solid shoals of fish herded about the seas like cattle, all of them seemed to have a cloak of semi-mystery flung about them, which a returning space-man like Dodge just wouldn't bother his head about.

The train snaked almost silently beneath the city, carrying them out beyond the parklike suburbs and the ring of factory-areas. Dodge leaned forward on the cushioned seat.

"Can you tell me anything of what this is all about?" he said pleasantly. "Grosvenor mentioned my Uncle Arthur and intimated that he was connected someway. Are you familiar with this—well . . ." he paused helplessly, and then said, with a half humorous chuckle: "with this case?"

She nodded. "I am. Fully. But Mr. Grosvenor expressly wishes to talk to you personally."

"Uh—it wouldn't be any good if I—no, I thought not." Dodge sat back. He crossed one knee over the other, and flicked his immaculate Space Navy Blacks into a leading-edge crease. From almost a lifetime in the Space Force, since his parents had died and he had replaced them with his ideals of a man's place out between the stars, his memory of Uncle Arthur, based on the half-dozen awkward meetings, was vivid. "Grosvenor said that Uncle Arthur had left me something, and I told him that all I expected was a bill for the drinks at the funeral. I told him I wasn't coming back to Earth just to collect a few thousand, or a decaying house." He looked puzzled. "Grosvenor said it wasn't a few thousand, and that the house was already decayed. What did he mean, Miss Tarrant?"

"I'm sorry. I am not at liberty to tell you." She sounded genuinely sorry, too, Dodge realized. The train ran out of the tunnel, nosing upwards to the terminus. People were rising, gathering their belongings, moving for the doors.

Just as Elise rose to her feet, she leaned forward, swaying slightly with the roll of the train, and Dodge, braced against his seat, felt the soft warmth of her body press for a heady moment against him. Then he heard her saying something, something that came in vagrant wafts of sound through the thunder of the blood in his temples.

"There is a great deal of injustice in the world. I mean real, brutal, callous, criminal injustice. You'll see. You might be able to do something about it, too." Then the train had stopped and the doors had opened and people were streaming for the escalators, and all Dodge could think about was the way Elise had crushed into him. Space makes a man sensitive to these things.

He stumbled along after her, pulling the black space bag free from the crowds jamming the escalator, and began to mull over her words. Injustice? Well, he supposed there was, although he'd not experienced any, except, perhaps, when they'd passed him over the first time for Lieutenant-Commander. But he had the idea that this strong-willed personality, thrusting ahead now, the shocking-pink sweater the target for many wolfish eyes, wouldn't consider for a micro-fraction of a second that as an example of injustice.

The terminus was a wide white sweep of concrete, flat roofed and with serpentine supporting pillars. Through the frame thus formed Dodge saw such a brilliance of sunshine that he blinked his eyes automatically. The air was crisp and biting, with a tang of ozone and bracing nippiness. They went with the crowd out and down the shallow steps, and there before him was the sea.

It was the first time in his life that he had seen the sea like this, standing on a low cliff-top, looking out across the white-flecked green and blue, and hearing the gentle susuration of shingled shores and feeling the good clean breeze blowing through the dusty pores of his body. Sea birds wheeled and screamed, their cries drifting down the air to him, their bodies minuetting through intricate, formal dances, suspended on curved brave wings against the sky.

"Surprised?" Elise said gravely.

"Yes." He decided to be honest. "Yes, I am. I'd no idea—it's beautiful."

"It holds its secrets well," she said cryptically.

Above them the sky was the faintest, translucent shade of blue, so brilliant that the mere air-glow hurt their eyes. The shining bowl seemed to surge away from them and, recurving, swoop in towards their feet so that the heavy green grass and rich earth of the cliff seemed suspended in an exquisite, precious and infinite globe of diluted light.

With a feeling almost of trespass, he began to follow Elise down the curved pathway to the foot of the cliffs. He'd seen the seas of Earth as few had seen them, gleaming mottled on the vast bulk of the planet, rushing up as his frail rocket fell headlong towards them. That had been a grand and wonderful experience, giving him, for a magic moment, a sense of superiority, of dispassionate calm removed from the troubles of the world. But this—this was on a different plane altogether. This sense of wonder that pervaded him now was his birthright, something that his ancestors had taken in joy for thousands of years; taken for granted, taken and moulded as their temperaments directed. And he, a child of Earth, was seeing it for the first time.

He began to appreciate an inkling of Elise's reaction to the Space Force. And then he shrugged off the whole mood and looked about him as he might have done stepping down from the landing ramp of his ship on any strange and alien planet.

The beach was an almost perfect arc of white sand. The sea laved it caressingly, without rancor, as though the titanic power of Neptune had been bridled and harnessed. Staring out to sea, he could just make out the long low dam which made that a fact, and no longer a fancy. This whole area of water before him was fenced off from the turbulence of the ocean. Across its bosom scudded yachts, trim shapes with pouter-pigeon spinnakers and stiff scraps of colored bunting at their trucks. Catamarans ploughed railway lines of foam and laughing people swallow-tailed in the wake of speedboats, miraculously supported on fragile skis that threw back the light of the sun in golden slivers of speed. Swimmers were everywhere. Their tanned arms flashed above the waves. Dodge saw with dumbfounded amazement a tot of no more than a year—certainly the little fellow could never yet have walked —calmly butterflying along and leaving a neat, precise wake of regularly spaced whirlpools. He shook his head and followed Elise onto the beach.

On the beach were six wooden shacks, painted in pastel colors, and with bright beach-balls and water-skis and aqua-floats and pedallers scattered casually around them.

Dodge looked. His mouth tightened up.

"Miss Tarrant. I came here to see Mr. Grosvenor. I do not see any hotel."

She gestured casually out towards the horizon. Dodge, impelled more by something within himself he could not explain, than the pointing arm, looked. Now that he stared closely, he could see bulges at intervals along the top of the mammoth sea wall. And there were other dark island specks here and there in the waters. But there was nothing which he could recognize as a hotel.

"Well?" he said, trying not to put too much acidity into his voice. He had to remember that he wasn't ordering a space cruiser's crew about. "I fail to see a hotel."

"It's out there, Commander," she said abstractedly. She had her head back and was squinting her eyes against the glare. She made an interesting profile; Dodge was more concerned, just at the moment, with finalizing this business and getting back to the Moon.

He said: "You drag me out here, promise me I'm going to meet Mr. Mystery-man Grosvenor at the Blue Deep Hotel and what hap . . ." He stopped. His mouth remained open foolishly. He swallowed.

"Blue Deep," Dodge said.

His voice was a squeak. He swallowed again and pointed out to sea.

"Blue Deep! Under the sea! Oh no! I'm not getting wet for you or twenty Grosvenors."

She laughed a little shamefacedly.

"It's not blue, as you can see. And it's not at all deep." She dimpled. "I thought you knew. Really I did. You see," she added in a rush. "Mr. Grosvenor spends all his time under, that is, all his time near here, and he's such a busy man that it saves a lot of time if he sees people at the Blue Deep. Neither of you have to come all the way then, you see," she finished practically. Dodge couldn't get the hang of that at all.

He said threateningly: "You're not enticing me to go down in a dratted submarine. The things are dangerous."

"Didn't you rocket out to Jupiter?"

"Yes. But that's different. We've organized . . ."

"Well, don't you think that the Navy have organized too?"

Dodge knew quite well that he was putting on an act and that any fears he had were quite unconnected with the mere fact of going under the sea. There was something very much adrift with this whole orbit, he sensed that, but quite naturally he didn't know what. If he did, now, well—he might go along with it, just for the company of Miss Elise Tarrant.

Yeah—he might, at that.

He persevered with the chit-chat. "When you're in a spaceship you've got the stars for company. When you're in a submarine you've only yourself—and, sister, that's bad."

She wasn't listening. She had her hands up shading her eyes and was peering into the sky again. Dodge looked up.

A bloated cigar of shining silver nosed daintily over the edge of the cliff and sailed out over the beach, gradually dropping towards the sand. A rope snaked from a cabin slung underneath forward and aft, and the whirling propellers on either side slowed, became visible and stopped. The airship touched down.

Laughing holiday-makers from the sands mixed with the ground crew tailing on the landing ropes. Everything seemed to be run on casual, democratic, no-fuss-no-rush lines. No one appeared to give orders, and yet the ship was streamlined into the wind, a ramp slid down, and the passengers tumbled off. Children were gamboling around, jumping up and down excitedly as their parents hauled a rope or handled the gangplank.

"That's an airship?" Dodge said in a strangled voice. "I thought they were deader than the galleys."

"Come on." Elise began to walk, sliding and plunging

16

in the sand, towards the airship. "I thought we might have missed it. We're just in time."

Dodge didn't argue. He was past that. If this sprite of a girl wanted him to stand on his head and recite the "Walrus and the Carpenter," he probably would—just for the laughs, though, he told himself sternly, just for the laughs.

The airship blossomed over his head as they came up to the ramp. A man with a straw Panama hat, a blue naval uniform jacket over bathing trunks, and sandals, smiled at them as they went aboard. They stood by a slanting window, watching the other people from the train coming aboard or making for the bar. No one asked them for a ticket or for money. Presently the ship lifted off, waved away by the happy bathers below, and slanted out towards the sea.

Dodge had noticed the words, twelve feet high—so he'd just been able to read them—on the flanks of the Zeppelin.

BLUE DEEP HOTEL.
BEST WATER IN SEVEN SEAS.

"How come the hotel runs an airship?" he asked.

They were sitting in the lounge by a window, the sea a glittering carpet of green and violet and blue below.

"We could have taken a helicopter or a flying-carpet or we could have gone by launch," Elise said matter-of-factly. "But the Blimp happened to be scheduled next. And I happen to like riding her. I like the sensation."

"Dirigible, not Blimp," Dodge said automatically. "Rigid construction. All right. Why not a submarine?"

"You won't get your ears wet, Commander. The hotel extends into the air, rising from the sea-bed, and you can descend right to the floor in air. It's most convenient."

"I happen to like breathing air," Dodge said. He meant it. Most of his pals who'd tried to breathe space had not come home to tell him about it. "How long do we take?"

"Fifteen minutes. It's not long."

"I still can't get over the idea of an underwater hotel running an airship for guests. All mixed up."

Elise favored him with one of her rare smiles.

"One word," she said sweetly. "Helium."

Dodge understood then; of course, it was a neat idea.

"We use helium in space, and divers and such use it— to stop getting drunk, isn't it?—and this ship makes a grand emergency reservoir."

"Not all emergency, either. They replenish from the ballonets when necessary, and the ship tanks up when she returns to the shore. Oh, and it's good publicity, too." She crinkled her nose, a gesture that Dodge was beginning to recognize. "How come you know about getting drunk?"

He tried to look injured. Playing the gay insouciant under these conditions of fresh experiences and a full sense of living—and a beautiful girl—was not at all difficult. "Drunk? Me? I'm strictly T.T., Miss, I'll have you know."

She didn't smile, though. She said: "I meant about your knowing that divers get drunk if they go deep—if they don't use helium."

Dodge happened to be following out of the corner of his eye the creamy wake of a double-decked catamaran below, and the craft swept out of sight below the window directly above Elise's hand, lying on the arm of her chair. Dodge saw that hand clench as she spoke, the knuckles go tallow white and shiny.

"Why," he said without betraying his growing unease in the odd little facets of this affair. "We had a job out on the Hartshorn Reef on Venus one time. The old *Arakan* went in with all jets blasting. Did a bit of salvage, adapting space gear. We knew about the effects of nitrogen— narcosis and pressure-illness—used to call it the 'bends'— but that's all."

"So you do know something of the undersea world," she said thoughtfully. "For a moment I thought—oh, well, never mind. We're here."

Dodge leaned forward over the table. "You thought I might be putting up a front, didn't you, Miss Tarrant? You thought I might not be Commander Jeremy Dodge, didn't you? You thought I might be someone else?"

CHAPTER TWO

Her reaction was shocking. Her face drained of color, leaving suddenly noticeable rings of purple beneath her eyes and lines of strain he had not noticed before. Her little gasp was not stopped as the tip of her tongue flicked into sight between her teeth. She was badly frightened.

Then she had recovered. She brushed a quick hand through her dark hair, tossing her head back, rising to her feet completely in control of herself again. But Dodge wasn't fooled. His suspicions crystallized. This girl was living under the weight of an oppressive fear, it had glared from her eyes in that moment of shocked unguardedness. And whatever she was frightened of was bad medicine for Jeremy Dodge; of that he was completely certain. It behooved him to be watchful.

The airship had been fastened to a mooring mast and now lay snuggled against it, head to wind, like an infant at a feeding tube. As they descended with the other passengers, this time in a smooth hydraulic lift, Dodge felt amazed at the casual tempo of life. Things got done, fast and efficiently, but there was no fuss, no shouting, no hallooing of orders and questions and counter-suggestions. It didn't seem to matter who did what, everything was performed good-naturedly and with a ready smile. Jokes flew thick and fast. If this was life on Earth—outside the cities—it seemed the best place possible for anyone to be. Dodge realized that it was the lack of strain; in space every moment might bring abrupt, awful danger; here on the quiet Earth people could go about their daily tasks without that ever-present sense of impending doom. You could be happy on Earth. It was quite a revelation. And against that bright background lay the stain of a girl's secret fear.

On the landing platform he turned towards the horizon, one hand still on the guard rail, feeling the breeze against his body and wondering just how near the retaining wall of the artificial lake the hotel lay. He looked across the long smooth swell of the open sea, empty and rolling under the sky. Clouds massed above like serrated leaves and a few birds skimmed low over the rollers. He whirled, fast. The wall lay a few hundred yards towards the shore, cutting off much of the lake from view; the white cliffs looked impossibly remote, like a streaming tail of cloud above the water.

"I told you it was called the Blue Deep," Elise said, realizing Dodge's reactions. "It's in the open sea—although on this coast that's as safe as behind the chicken wire."

Dodge let that pass. They went down into the hotel depths. The building was a ring, two hundred yards across, built upon the solid rock of the sea floor, its four upper storys and the landing platform above the waves, the rest of its bulk wrapped in two hundred and fifty feet of water. The walls were transparent and cunning lighting fixtures had been positioned outside, so that a deep green luminescence filled the descending spiral of the stairway surrounding the inner lobbies and rooms and restaurants.

People swarmed everywhere. And yet there was not that insufferable crush that Dodge had experienced with irritation in the city. Men and women wearing only the briefest of trunks and bras and transparent capes moved leisurely up and down. Many carried swimming flippers and face masks. Tiny children, stark naked, ran and squealed and queued up in fighting bundles for preference at the air-locks up and down the hotel's walls. Husky, broad-shouldered, good-looking youths, with 'Lifeguard' stenciled all over them, tried to instill some discipline into the kids, and others marshaled parties, equipped with sling-shots and spring-guns and compressed-air harpoons, for underwater hunting expeditions. Studious-looking highbrows wandered about with a profusion of camera and sketching equipment waterproofed for underwater use. Giggling girls, who were clearly—and so rightly—prime exponents of the back-to-nature movement, waved to friends gliding gracefully past the windows outside. Out there a bubbling, squirming, contorting class of neophytes was going through its paces under the eyes of watchful instructors. Elise sniffed scornfully.

"Even though this is a make-believe deep-sea hotel," she said disdainfully, "at least it is more adventurous than those within the chicken wire. And that's where those dry-necks belong."

From one airlock protruded the stern of a submarine, with excited passengers taking their places within.

"Joy rides round the reef," said Elise.

They passed into a wide hall where comfortable foam plastic chairs were ranged before a single vast sheet of clear plastic let into the outside wall. Throbbing music permeated the warm air. Outside, in the limpid water, whole chorus lines of girls were going through their routine, their liquid bodies flowing through the water as though part of it. They were wearing gleaming, reflecting, tinsel costumes and the patterns they created were almost hypnotic. Dodge had to tear his eyes away and follow Elise through the rear of the auditorium.

This wasn't just a new life—this was a whole new world.

At the reception desk, flooded in mellow artificial light, Elise spoke to the girl. The receptionist had red hair, and its coiffed waves were interlaced with sea-shells and pearls and star-fish. Everywhere Dodge looked the motif was one of marine life. Etched into plastic wall panels, moulded around lamp fittings, painted in sweeping frescoes on the ceilings, patterned in the rugs, all the mysterious life of the sea was illuminated and invigorated by a master hand.

"Oh dear," Elise said, turning to Dodge. "I'm sorry, Commander. Mr. Grosvenor has gone on a hunt. He wasn't really expecting you until later, you know."

"I don't know." Dodge felt annoyed. "Well, how long will he be?"

She didn't flush, but her eyebrows arched fractionally. As she spoke, Dodge felt a heel.

"He has gone with an inner-wall party to watch a new consignment of dentex—that's a small carnivorous fish—and they may be out some time. There's a chance that they will go on to hunt in one of the preserves."

Dodge nodded grumpily and spotted a passing waiter. He attracted the man's attention, trying not to be disconcerted by his waiter's uniform of bathing trunks and black bow-tie.

"Bring me a whisky, please," he said.

Elise spoke quickly.

"Ah—er . . . I wouldn't, Commander."

Dodge was dumbfounded.

"What goes on here, Miss Tarrant? Are you some sort of wet-nurse or something? Look—I'm not a habitual drunk. I can drink a single whisky now and again without ill effects, you know." He couldn't resist adding: "Your honor will still be safe."

As soon as he'd said it he wished he hadn't.

Thankfully enough, she let it ride. "Look, Commander, there's a small underwater châlet out where Mr. Grosvenor is hunting. I know you're in a hurry"—Dodge grunted at this—"so I suggest we both fly out there now. We can catch an aquaplane easily."

For a moment Dodge considered.

"All right. You've brought me this far on this will o' the wisp chase. I might as well go the full distance. What is this aquaplane?"

She dimpled. "You'll see. If you'll register—you'll have to stay the night now—we can go straight to the dressing rooms and airlock. I have a room here."

After he had purchased a pair of swimming trunks and been shown into his room where he found a standard of comfort he had not expected, he changed and went quickly through the other residents to the dressing rooms, conscious of his space-pallor. His white skin stood out like a lump of chalk in a poppy-field.

The dressing room was an oblong chamber with one side studded with the inner valves of airlocks. The opposite wall contained a long counter, behind which stood attendants and racks of flippers, face masks, underwater hunting weapons, cameras, lines, all the impedimenta that a person might want to take into the sea. A helpful attendant was quickly persuaded by Dodge that a Commander in the Space Force knew all about living under alien conditions, and that he had no need of special tuition.

Dodge hired a pair of plastic flippers and put them on gingerly, trying to appear nonchalant. He was just reaching forward to take a face mask when a cool voice came from the region of his right ear.

"All ready to go, Commander? Good."

He turned.

He had had enough shocks this day to last him quite a time. But he'd experienced nothing to compare with this. What he saw convinced him that he'd been wasting his time in space—he should have been with Elise Tarrant a very long while ago. A very long while indeed. A panicky thought crossed his mind. Suppose she were married?

She was smiling at him, and he saw at once that she was just a little uneasy at the impression she was creating.

Her bathing costume was a brilliant, livid scarlet. It consisted of a narrow string supporting a wedge-shaped flame of scarlet and two small cups of scarlet plastic. It hid just enough to rank as clothes—and did what clothes always can do to a woman. As for the rest of Miss Tarrant—well, Dodge passed a dry tongue across his lips and became slowly aware that she was, at last, blushing.

He took his eyes, that felt as though they were on stalks, away and mumbled something about being sorry, and then realized sinkingly, that that made it worse.

He searched frantically for something to say.

Picking up the face mask he said, inanely: "Where are the air cylinders?"

Elise seized the change of conversations—Dodge's silent admiration had been all the more vocal for being dumb —and busily pulled forward her own mask. She pointed to the cheekpieces.

"These are the cylinders. We use spun glass-fibre and plastic—much stronger than steel for holding compressed gases—and the pressure is a lot of atmospheres. They don't use liquid oxy up here. The pressure demand regulator here"—she touched the round machined-box at the nape of the mask fastenings—"is a quadruple effect regulator.

Brings that pressure of air in the flasks down through four stages until it reaches the pressure of the surrounding water. Then you breathe it."

She had talked out the by-play, and now Dodge felt more composed. It was a hell of a jolt to turn round to see a girl like that at your elbow. He wished he knew more about her. Some of the things she said would bear closer inspection. How could this hotel be "up" here?

He looked at the cheekpieces, saw that they were small cylinders with re-inforced corrugated tubes, running from either side, to a mouthpiece with a rubber grip for the teeth.

The attendant, a husky negro with a grin that split his face in two and a torso that could have held Atlas and the world, had watched the meeting of Elise and Dodge and now he coughed discreetly. Dodge remembered that he was supposed to be an underwater expert. He tried to be clever.

"In the Space Force we have the intake and mask in one," he said loftily. "None of this gripping onto it with your teeth, frightened to spit it out."

Elise jumped in with both flippers.

"The Space Force work under nil pressure," she said twisting the mask in her hand. "Carbon di-oxide exhaled through the nose goes viscous under pressure and hangs around poisoning you. So we make the places where it can collect as small as possible. That's why."

Dodge felt as small as he knew he deserved to feel.

He turned away from the counter and began to walk towards the airlock.

"Your radio, sir," the attendant said in his melodious Southern voice.

Dodge picked up the little transceiver and then went off stumbling in the flippers and allowed Elise to show him how it fitted on the mask. A simple throat microphone and amplifier connected to a diaphragm which would be in direct contact with the water, he reckoned that it would be good for a few feet communication submerged. With the understanding that you couldn't keep up a sustained conversation with a mouthpiece between your lips, he was beginning to see that there was more to this sub-aqua stuff than he had realized. He had previously thought that you simply transferred proved space techniques underwater; but he had to admit that there was more to it than that. It was the pressure. They'd found out a bit about that on the Hartshorn Reef, on Venus.

When his gear was stowed all about him—they didn't take harpoon guns, much to Dodge's secret disappointment —he went with Elise over to the airlocks. They waited their turn and as they were stepping over the wet gratings, Elise suddenly took his arm and spoke softly into his ear.

"Oh, Commander, I should have warned you. The water may be a trifle cold to you. We're going inside the chicken wire and they warm it up there with a net-work of heaters along the bottom. If you just let yourself go and strike out with your feet we'll soon be in the warm."

Then the valve had closed at their backs and the water began to rise around their feet. The six other people in the lock, young couples, were already skylarking around.

Warm the water! That must be quite an engineering proposition, Dodge summed up, trying to distract his mind from the air he was sucking into his mouth and the slight pressure of the mask and the weight of the gear and most especially of the water rising inexorably around his thighs and stomach and chest. It seemed an age before the outer lock opened and they were through. Immediately outside was a caged platform and here attendants, masked and flippered like themselves, attached weights and adjusted their buoyancy. Dodge just hung in the water.

It was cold.

Damned cold.

Goose pimples started up at once, telling Dodge that his first layer of insulation had gone down. He thrashed with his legs and shot forward. Elise's voice, faintly amused, came bubblingly but clearly through the water.

"You're going the wrong way, Commander. Over here."

He tried to turn, and felt the mask biting into his face. She must have spotted this.

"Breathe out from your nose. That'll equalize the pressure and stop the mask cutting your face off."

He did so and the pressure vanished. He waggled his flippers. Sensations attacked him from all sides simultaneously. The feeling of floating, of being buoyed up, was quite familiar to a man who had lived out weeks of free-fall. But he ran into one profound difference immediately.

He tried to flip himself round to face towards Elise as he would have done in space. Everything happened except what he wanted. It felt as though he were trying to force himself through a planet-sized treacle tart with a child's pusher for weapon. He thrashed wildly with his arms, afraid to move his feet for fear of shooting off at some fresh impossible tangent.

For one horrible moment he had the feeling that he was buried alive.

"Hold steady," Elise's voice through the water was full of laughter, of impish hilarity. That acted like a tonic on Dodge. "Just let yourself hang, keep still. Then we'll try some exercises."

He refused to be needled. Obediently he stopped moving. He knew enough about this business of pressure to swallow to clear his Eustachian tubes, at least to open them so that air pressure could meet and balance the outside water pressure on his ear drums. So far he hadn't spoken a word; now, he articulated through the throat mike: "How deep are we?"

Elise had a depth meter strapped to her wrist. She said, without looking at it: "Forty feet. Nothing at all, except for pressure variations. Now, if you'll just lie like a log I'll tow you across to an aquaplane—there's one just ready to go."

Fuming, embarrassed by his own suddenly demonstrated incompetence, and yet annoyingly and humiliatingly pleased by the sybaritic feeling of the girl towing him in smooth undulating surges through the water, Dodge relaxed and was towed. He had forgotten the last time he had felt so utterly helpless before purely physical conditions; it was all a trick, of course, a matter of adjustment. His almost symbiotic relationship with spatial conditions, leading to an automatic reaction, had betrayed him here in this underwater realm. He'd learn.

The aquaplane was a hydrodynamic wing surface, with rudder and diving planes controlled by a joystick. The pilot reclined in the center at the controls. From the trailing edges of the wing, lengths of rope were hanging, with ring-handles, at their ends. Already two or three couples had hung on, looking like trapeze artists warming up for the show. Elise deftly slid sideways, freeing Dodge, and all in the same motion, thrusting a pair of rings into his hands. He grasped them, watching her take the adjacent pair and turn a laughing face towards him.

Laughing? Yes—she blew a big bubble of air at him and then replaced her mouthpiece. Big joke. Great fun. Dodge turned his facemask the other way sourly, and watched as the pilot fiddled with his controls. As Elise and he had hooked on, the pilot glanced to his rear, then looked forward again. The cable, which looped from the aquaplane's bow and disappeared upwards into color-shot haze, shivered its sinuous length, straightened, and then as the aquaplane gathered momentum, relaxed again into its graceful curve. The whole traveling circus moved through the water, towed, Dodge surmised, by a motor boat on the surface above their heads.

To his left the water was a glowing sheet of color from the levels of the hotel windows and the outside lights. Its transparency surprised him. Somehow, underwater, he had expected to see, and be continually reminded of the liquid element; he found that it was like space in that he saw through it, and the objects within his field of vision attracted his attention far more than the substance—or lack of it—in which they were embedded. Seeing was particularly good. His spirits began to rise as he felt the forward motion of his body, balancing the unease he felt, occasioned not least by the irrational feeling of pressure on his body. He was under a pressure of three atmospheres down here, but, for all the feeling of difference it made, it could have been thirty-three.

He suddenly felt bad at snubbing Elise, and turned to her. He was just about to phrase a carefully noncommittal sort of remark, when he felt the forward movement of his body pulling him up on the aquaplane. The lights of the hotel had vanished; before him reared a huge rectangle of yellow light, outlining a smaller oval of light. The aquaplane slowed before the oval, which Dodge saw indistinctly was the entrance to a tunnel.

Elise said sharply: "Double up and decelerate, Commander. We're going through the lock."

27

How it was done, Dodge didn't know. One moment he was freezing in the open sea, the next, he was blindly following the aquaplane, with its tow-rope sliding through a slit in the roof, and emerging into a brightly-lit area where the water was of a heavenly warmth. He shivered in involuntary reaction.

The pilot glanced behind again, then a number of small plane-shaped rectangles of plastic drifted back on lines from the wing. Elise shook her head. The next pair of rings supported a young Siamese girl. She caught the horizontal bar of the plane, released the rings and then swept away behind the aquaplane. Dodge lay over on his side to watch.

The girl handled the little plane superbly. She twisted the bar, the plane dipped and she went swooping down until all that Dodge could see was the descending rope. Then she rose into vision again, hair a flying cloud as she braked and turned her triangular face towards her companion. He took off in a second plane, rising and falling in a series of controlled plunges; the girl tried a complicated maneuver to avoid him, and the next second they were both spiraling and spinning away beyond the limits of vision.

"It's grand fun, Commander. But you're in a hurry, you say?"

"That's right. Is it much further?"

"Not far. This water is all plankton free—they like it like that for clarity—but they have to provide food for the fish at regular intervals." She pointed with one hand. "Otherwise the fish just wouldn't stay around. Over there you'll see the wire soon. Preserves. Various kinds, hunting, photography, breeding. All very scientific."

At odd moments they passed spheres of light, suspended in the water by their own balanced buoyancy. It was as light as day beneath the surface. It was all very pleasant, very refreshing, very exciting, really; and yet Dodge could not throw off that feeling of depression, of savage refusal to accept things at their face value, a mood, almost of masochism.

Just sour grapes, he supposed, because Elise was so perfectly at home underwater and had no hesitation about helping him like a lame dog—which was pretty thick, when he thought about it. Out in space, with the clear clean sweep of the stars for company, he could feel at home. Down here, paddling around like a shrimp in a pool, he felt shut off, trapped; with all his freedom of movement and a knowledge of the vastness of the oceans, he had a strong sensation of claustrophobia. Get this interview over with—and he'd have his bath walled up and use the shower from now on.

Elise waved to the pilot and said to Dodge: "Let go, Commander. We're here. Keep your body still and just waggle your feet up and down. I'll guide you."

Manfully, Dodge did not reply but did as he was directed. Rather to his own surprise, he found himself moving after Elise, a little uncertainly, true, and with many a wobble and convulsion to regain his original direction; but he was proceeding—and learning.

Elise caught the wire—close meshed and triple reinforced—hung on and waited for him. She was looking all about her, expectantly, Dodge thought. He could see no sign of an opening and was just about to enquire sarcastically whether she thought he could emulate an eel as well as a fish, when three dark shadows slipped down towards him. For a single instant panic threatened to whelm him; then he recovered shakily, as he saw Elise's vivid scarlet bathing costume in almost its true brilliant color, from a drifting globe of yellowish-white light. The shadows resolved into men with face masks, flippers and harpoon guns.

They swam, Dodge saw, with prodigious ease, swinging high over Elise and swooping down towards her. She lifted her hand. The men by some subtle shift of direction angled directly towards him. Fractionally, as they surged towards him like three torpedoes homing on an unwanted asteroid, he caught sight of something he did not understand and could not believe.

Then the first man had grasped Dodge's arms, the second his legs and the third raced in towards his side.

Dodge shouted—got a mouthful of water and felt his mouthpiece thrust clumsily back into position. He felt the prick in his arm quite distinctly.

Hypodermic.

Even then some wayward thought tried to work out

the pressure-resistant qualities a hypo would need for underwater use. Even as the answer that it was easy came, he felt the first surges of blackness taking over. He tried to move his legs, his arms, but they were weighted with all the lead on the Moon. Sparks swam across his eyes. He felt a grip tighten across his chest.

Just before the final blackness and deep oblivion came down like night on Mercury, he saw that what he had not believed was true.

These three men had facemasks over their eyes—but they didn't have any air tanks that he could see. There were no mouthpieces in their mouths—and those mouths were wide open to the sea water.

Dodge, firmly convinced that he was having a nightmare, blacked out.

CHAPTER THREE

Within and about, the water flow moved with the gentle, profound, deliberate movements of ages of ritual, and centuries after centuries of habit that not even Man with his brash and energetic intrusion could alter or modify. Within the living rock, air spaces, bubbles of an alien element, warred continually with the thrusting pressure of the sea. Men and women, no less fishlike than the creatures that swam and drifted far above them, pursued their own familiar ways of life and created a haven, a simulacrum of the upper world; here on the sea bed six hundred feet down and two hundred miles from the shore line, where at last the patient land could shake the sea from his hoary shoulders and rise into the sunlight.

Simon Hardy exhaled gustily and dropped onto the bench from which he could study the TV screen on the far wall.

"Another one!" he said.

"We can't be sure yet." Pierre Ferenc gestured toward the screen. Its gray, lifeless face stared back. "They may have had a breakdown."

Hardy grunted. He had a fine-carved face like a teak figurehead of some old clipper ship, with close-cropped white hair that covered his skull like a helmet. His eyes were a pale, washed-out violet, and he had a habit of clutching his jaw, as square and arrogant as a spiked helmet, with the blunt fingers of his right hand. His left arm ended at the elbow. That had been a shark, before Hardy had triggered the second harpoon. He didn't bother too much about it now, and kept a couple of prosthetic limbs somewhere in a cupboard.

"Sure they've had a breakdown—the same damned breakdown the other three subs had." He looked at Ferenc critically. The youngster was a good aide, valuing the power of optimism and yet with a strong, practical streak behind that classic profile and that wavy hair. He must be about due to be made up to Captain by this time. Hardy himself thought he must be making Admiral of the Fleet soon; but no one bothered overmuch about rank down here. The job was what mattered. And the job wasn't going right. This was the fourth deep-sea sub that had failed to return, and for all the good the direct communications-link he had ordered set-up on the personal ultra-sonic TV screen was doing, he might as well be out hunting sea-urchins.

In abrupt negation of that bitter thought, a voice spurted from the speaker grille.

"D.S. Nine calling N.O.P. Trident. Conditions emergency. Will try to connect outside pickup. Conditions emergency. Looks as though we've had it."

The screen wavered with a pale green luminescence. Both Hardy and Ferenc leaned forward, breathing lightly, not speaking. The picture was badly defined. Blobs of color gyrated, lights flickered, throwing momentary impressions of the sleek side of the deep-sea sub into shining relief. Then a single light source grew, steadied, showed the forward fins of the ship with the exterior harpoon gun cradled low on the deck in the foreground. Out beyond the prow, indistinct, infuriating in their vagueness, small forms hovered, and swooped, closing up until they were almost distinguishable and then retreating with the impression of flauntingly insolent fins.

"Not men," Ferenc said.

The voice from the speaker chattered. "Something's knocking on the hull!" The sheer terror in the voice turned Hardy's face to granite. "Outside. Trying to get in. And we're at Mermaids twelve!" The clear sound of a gulp across those miles of icy water. "I'll try to shift record to other pickups."

The screen went crazy, then dissolved back to its featureless gray. Time ticked away.

"No go, I'm afraid. Whoever's outside doesn't want to pose for photographs." The voice had regained some semblance of humanity. The sub-officer down there had faced his own moment of truth and had come through, with the knowledge that he and his crew were doomed, and that, if they were going to die anyway, they might as well send as much information back as they could. They knew their friends would be diving down into these depths again, following them.

"Mermaids fourteen, now. We're not under control of the fins. Propulsors stopped a while ago. I don't think I'm crazy; and yet I unhesitatingly say that we are being taken somewhere by someone—or something—outside." The voice was calm, steady. The screen flicked back to the first view, and now Hardy saw the sudden boiling away of slender fins as the light over the camera came on. In the distance—a matter of ten feet at that depth and with that light source—he thought he caught a glimpse of a gleaming silver shape that reminded him of something he should have recognized at once, and yet, which remained tantalizingly beyond the grip of his memory.

"Mermaids fifteen and a half. The old Nine will take twenty without too much trouble—the snag is that the bottom is twenty-five, or thereabouts, here. I think we'll crush flatter than a steam-rollered toothpaste-tube." There was nothing now in the young voice from the speaker to tell what he was thinking. Hardy could guess. Twenty-five thousand feet down in the sea. Waiting, with the steady merciless upward sweep of the depth-needle; he felt connected in that waiting by his own waiting, with the thrum of the recording camera over his shoulder, storing up the last moments of the sub and her men. He wished he could sweat naturally.

What happened was not pretty.

The Juliana Trench—a monstrous gash in the sea bed, five hundred miles long, a score wide and 25,000 feet deep at its greatest depth—lay across the southerly-routed trade lines like a great dike. Surface liners ploughed the waves far above it, scarcely conscious of its existence, except for the sudden sharp lines recorded on their echo sounders. Submarines had penetrated to its lip, and nosed over, sliding silently above the black abyss yawning below. And now, Deep Sub Nine had ventured too far down, had been—caught?—by some malignant force dwelling deep in the cold, black fastnesses of that huge crevice in the Earth's crust. Simon Hardy felt like an old man, crushed in spirit as Nine was crushed in metal and plastic. The last moments were spent, after the outside pickup finally blew in under pressure, with a hastily rigged camera, relaying dial and meter information back to Under Ocean Patrol Base Trident.

Nine took twenty-three thousand five hundred feet before the screen went black.

"Why do we do it?" Ferenc was saying. He had lost comrades on Nine. "Why do we have to go down into the sea? We were made for sun and air and the breezes of Earth . . ."

"One phrase, Pierre," Hardy said harshly. "Self respect. Man must know that he is master on his own planet. Whilst those depths are there, we will descend into them. Just as we must climb the mountains on the roof of the world, just because they are there. Man cannot afford to be afraid of the dark corners of his planet."

"We've had equipment to reach those depths safely for years," Ferenc burst out. "There's something down there, some horrible force that sucks men down . . ."

"All right!" Hardy re-channeled the ultra-sonic TV set personally. "I'm going to speak to Henderson. There'll be hell to pay when UN hears about this."

The ultra-sonic waves from the undersea fortress were translated into radio waves by the automatic slave transmitter bobbing in the swell on the surface, beamed to UN Headquarters. Ocean Secretary Henderson answered at once in response to the call from the Head of Under Ocean Patrol. Henderson was small and compact, a lithe dynamo of a man who possessed a computer for a brain and statistical index for a heart. What he wanted, he persuaded other people to get for him. Now, his thin, intense face creased by lines of worry; he exploded into excited comment when Hardy had finished speaking.

"The Board won't like this, Simon. There's too much money being thrown away. Lord knows I go along with your schemes . . ."

"Not just my schemes, Henderson. Everyone needs what we plan, even though they don't realize it. If Earth is to feed herself, we must keep the Bishop Wilkins projects going, but we must also conquer the whole ocean. We know that is essential."

Henderson nibbled his lip. "I know you're right, Simon. But sometimes I wonder. Toxter of the Space Board was in to see me earlier. He means to fight. They want a whole heap of appropriations—fantastic sums—for the assault on Saturn. UN can't keep too many balls in the air at the same time. Someone's going to get the thin edge of the wedge."

"You mean they'll cut down our deep-sea appropriations?"

"We must continue with the Patrol's main function, to guard and protect the interests of the Wilkins farms. Yes, I think the deep-sea projects may have to be shelved. I don't know, Simon, I just don't know." Henderson forced a smile. "If you could lay before the board some successes—this is the fourth sub to disappear, isn't it?"

Hardy was emphatic. "Tell the board that we have reason to believe that there is—something—down in the sea. Something that can drag a submarine down to death. That should shake them out of their complacency."

"But, Simon, don't you see. Whatever is down there —and we've no real proof, remember—must have been down there a long while. It hasn't bothered us before. Only when we probe down there ourselves . . ."

"You mean we should let sleeping dogs lie?"

"Nothing fresh on the scattering layers?" Henderson replied obliquely.

"No," Hardy said shortly. "Subs report nothing when they reach the depth. But as soon as they leave we get the same echoes—as though they'd sunk onto a patch of oil and thrust it away from all about them." There was urgency in his voice. "I'm convinced that the two phenomena are related."

CITY UNDER THE SEA

Ferenc moved uneasily in the background, then stilled at Hardy's impatient wave. Far away on the surface Henderson warmed to his main theme.

"Now look, Simon. I can't promise anything about deep-sea just now. I think it would be wiser if you did not send any more deep-sea subs out." He licked his lips. "I've had disturbing reports from plenty of continental shelves. The North sea is pretty quiet—their production is well above schedule. It's not so good on the Eastern American Banks, and some of the Pacific coasts are losing men by droves, in broad daylight. This kidnapping has got to stop! It's your job to ensure the corporations run an equitable and fair underwater industry. This press-ganging is getting up the noses of the whole UN, Simon, and Under Ocean is beginning to stink all over the world."

Hardy did not answer.

Henderson went on: "There's even been a rumor circulating that a movement is afoot to close down some of the Wilkins colonies. They say the money would be better spent putting Man on Saturn's satellites."

"What would they eat when they got there?" Hardy asked contemptuously. "Look, Henderson—I don't have to convince you that is a crass policy—and I shouldn't have to take it from you like a big stick. I'm doing all I can do with the resources at my disposal. The force is far too small. Some of the corporations have miles of continental shelf honeycombed with air and water spaces. As soon as a patrol puts its nose in all the slave labor is hustled away. The trim, well-fed volunteers work around until the patrol leaves, then the press-ganged poor devils are hauled out and set to work."

"Can't you insinuate . . ." Henderson began.

Hardy flicked a finger and Ferenc slid a film pack into the projector.

"Watch this, Henderson," Hardy said grimly.

Henderson's screen took on the green luster of the sea below the sixty feet mark, where the reds and oranges of the spectrum had been washed out. A vertical rock face covered the right hand side of the screen, and from this wall trailed the familiar profusion of underwater fronds, a fantastic welter of struggling life; many-branched gorgonians, looking blue and dark when Henderson knew they were really a flaming crimson, sea urchins prickling at the passage of swarms of erratic fish, their limpid bodies cavorting in every direction as they fled at the approach of a monster of the deep.

He was a man—rather, he had been a man.

His facemask covered his features; but the signs of privation, of incredible suffering, were written large on the rest of his body. His flippers moved sluggishly, painfully; he crept through the water like a half-crushed snail. He was wearing a vest that, at the depth, appeared green, and emblazoned across the chest was an interlinked monogram formed from the letters A.D.W.C. One leg twisted unnaturally and refused to propel him evenly through the water; he sagged drunkenly from side to side, and he had trouble adjusting his buoyancy.

"He got into the Artful Dodger's little lot," Hardy said flatly. "This is what they did, purely as normal routine, before he escaped. He was with them a month. That's all."

From both sides of the screen members of the U.O.P. swept forward, their tall conical helmets up and the slats opened. They took the injured man in their arms, flew swiftly with him past the camera, which panned to follow them into the airlock concealed under outgrowths of coral on the reef wall.

No air bubbled from the lock as the valves closed. Men under the sea who needed air didn't waste it. The camera stayed on the valve for an instant, and then the screen went gray; but Henderson could still see the broken harpoon standing up, like some obscene cocktail-stick, from the broad back of the man who had limped home from the sea.

Ferenc's hands were trembling as he shut off the projector. A quiet settled on the room deep beneath the sea, and a stillness, for a moment, held the room far away in UN Headquarters. Then Henderson spoke, and his voice was rough with passion.

"I'd no idea. Artful Dodger, I saw that. All right." His nostrils dilated. "We'll prosecute. Right away."

"What on?" Hardy said wearily. "No evidence. He couldn't bring any back, and he died without telling me much I didn't know." He gestured tiredly. "All the Wilkins Corporations are the same; you must know that. Undersea Oils aren't so bad; they need skilled men."

"Any poor drunken fool can look after fish!" Ferenc put in viciously. Neither of the others looked at him.

"I thought for a while last week that we might have trouble with those new manganese mines they've begun on Tsori Guyot in the middle of the Pacific. A native village was cleaned out, all the strong young men were taken." Hardy's lined face betrayed little feeling. "We traced it to a Halaokan Wilkins Corporation. We managed to return most of them; some died. It wasn't nine thousand feet down, like the manganese Guyot; but pressure fluctuation got them. The Halaokan people were using primitive equipment—sheer murder."

"If this stuff gets out to the Press," Henderson said, his face stiff, "they'll crucify us! I knew things were bad; but not like this. Toxter would bellow like a bull and spray pieces of U.O.P. all the way to Saturn."

"We need more appropriations, not less," Hardy said. "What do those space boys expect to do out on Saturn? Play hoops with the rings?"

Henderson gestured vaguely. "Expansion of Man's frontiers." The way he said it sounded like bubbling lava.

"We've fought a long struggle for undersea development, you and I," Hardy remarked, almost noncommitally. "I think we've one last throw before us. We daren't let any news of the way the Wilkins Corporations are acting leak out until the time is ripe; then we reveal enough to secure a revulsion of feeling."

"That's what we want to avoid, isn't it?" Henderson knew enough about his old friend to scent a plot.

"Yes. And this way we'll get what we want. We'll scare the pants off Toxter and all the bemedalled space boys."

"I don't quite see . . ."

Hardy explained. Not fully—his own ideas were still nebulous—but enough so that when he had finished talking, Henderson was more than half won over. The Ocean Secretary and Simon Hardy had bullied and cajoled UN into granting charters to private corporations, so that rapid development of continental shelves, and expansion of agriculture should not be held up. Whatever evils were inherent in such a scheme, they had felt at the time, would be more than compensated for by the immediate increase in land availability in aquiculture, and an upswing in the production of food and raw materials, of oil and minerals. And they had been right. Huge combines had been formed to exploit the sea bed. Literally hundreds of small private companies had sprung up, taking out a patent on a few hundred acres of continental shelf; working them under the aegis of UN, with limited resources, and often with primitive and dangerous undersea equipment.

But the bold gamble had paid off.

Now the landside received over half its food from sources under the sea. The Bishop Wilkins undersea farms spread and grew, fish pens and corrals and canneries bloomed between the edge of the shelf and the coast. The wealth of the seas lay open to humanity.

But the small companies were gradually taken over by the large; the same old story of land development followed. Frontier battles against an alien element took place side by side—and depth below depth—the board-room struggles for shares and control, debentures and stock interests. While men with aqualungs dived deep to tend the harvest of the seas other men, men with different visions and different values, sat and schemed, and inevitably abuses began, slowly at first, and then, as the difficulty of effectively controlling sea exploitation became monstrously apparent, sprang into world-wide scandal.

A scandal that lay only in the balance sheets of the corporations, and the inhuman controls of the aqualunging foremen, and the bewildered relatives of people reported as "missing."

A man can be broken very easily when he is alone under the sea.

And now, with the menfish, the problem had grown abruptly acute. Now, the corporations knew they stood without the law, and were glad because of it. They knew they could afford to go to any lengths, now, to obtain recruits. And U.O.P. sculled around, attempting the impossible task of policing eight million square miles, all the vast area of new lands of the continental plateaux under the sea.

"All right, Simon," Henderson said at last. "All right. We'll play it your way for now." His smile was warm and friendly. "But God help you if it goes wrong—because no one else will."

CHAPTER FOUR

Man moved into the sea. Man retraced the trail of ancestors that had flopped, near drowning in air, onto the warm mud inter-tidal flats, escaping from the ferocious enemies of the deep; crawling on paddle fins out into a new world, and a heritage that would not stop at the stars.

But before Man could take up the challenge of those winking spots of light that he had never seen in the seas, he must return to the womb he had spurned, and gather his resources there, garner the harvests of his ancestral home, feed and grow strong for the long, silent journeys between the stars.

He never felt it coming. Two things coincided and gave him a moment of sheer hell. The roller must have been a big one, deep and smooth and shining green with foam flecked flanks. And his air-tubes and valves stuck fractionally, as they so often seemed to do, and this time stayed stuck.

Scotomata flashed and flared before his eyes. His head felt as though someone was trying to wrench it off.

Then Harp thumped his tubes, freeing the valves, the roller took its sudden pressure imbalance away, and Dodge struggled with the suicidal desire to vomit. Being sick underwater was a one way trip to hell.

Not, he thought dully, that he wasn't in hell right now.

Why not just spit out the mouthpiece? Some men did. Some men refused any more to fly among the algae, through the rich weeds, the mutated plants, refused to herd fish for another moment. It would be so easy—just to push with his tongue and spit . . . Harp banged him cheerfully on the shoulder and waggled his fingers, thumb up. Dodge nodded back and his old purpose surged back, ten-fold reinforced by this momentary lapse. He was getting out of this watery grave, was flying back to the surface, was crawling out and tearing off his flippers and mask and was going gunning for Miss Elise Tarrant . . .

Harp motioned towards the shoal, their silvery bodies alive with twisting reflections from thinly scattered lamps. The control tower up ahead was emitting its pinging warning signal; soon now the polarity of the current would be switched and all the fish, like one, would turn tail and begin blindly swimming back the way they had come, greedily gobbling up the carefully distributed food from the men's packs.

Then, when he and Harp had reached the further end of the enormous netted area, they would not obey the warning ping from the tower and retrace their course, feeding the fish; no—they would slide through the hole they had cut with such infinite patience and strike out for the shore and freedom.

It had not been easy making all the plans. It hadn't been easy obtaining the wire cutters. But Harp and he had managed it, and they now both had the same flame of anger burning in them, the raging fury to return and revenge themselves on the authors of their mutual misery.

He could still recall the misery of his awakening, his first shocked awareness of his surroundings. His last thought had been of nightmare, of seeing men swimming with open mouths deep beneath the sea. And all of Elise Tarrant's veiled hints and oblique remarks had boiled up to a mushroom explosion in his mind. Since that moment of awakening in the locker rooms of this Wilkins Corporation, he had fanned that flame of anger, had known he was near insane with a rending, futile rage against the girl who had arranged for his kidnapping.

She must have organized it. There was no other explanation. Even the scarlet flame of her bathing costume was a part of the plot; Dodge remembered vividly the white light that had blazed on them, throwing colors into their true place in the spectrum. The scarlet scraps of dress and the white flame of the body within—what an utter fool he had been! Reacting like the standard female-starved dope off the spaceways, avidly following the luring flower of a woman's body straight into the jaws of hell. He'd reacted as planned, all right. And so here he was, prisoned beneath the sea.

Remembering that, Dodge's muscles lumped along his jaw. They had given him a face mask and flippers and driven him out into the water, pressuring him just as the water pressured him; and he had nothing—then—to resist as the air within his body resisted. He had waited. Biding his time. They had set him to clearing up slimy old beds of algae, clearing them with a short-handled rake. His stomach revolted at the job. A short course, in an air-space beneath a dome, convinced him that the work out in the sea was preferable to a rubber truncheon.

That was their simplest remedy for recalcitrants. The old Nazi *totschläger*—only they didn't quite beat to death. They caused pain. Pain that made work out on the razor-sharp coral reefs, among the poison-ivy of the sea and the merciless fire-coral, almost a pleasure. That was their simplest remedy. They had others.

Dodge had seen a man dragged fainting from a sandless tank, after a deliberately goaded venomous weever fish had finished with him.

There were other pleasures indulged in by the agile-minded guardians of the human fish-fodder working around the reefs, and out on the sea beds sweeping away to the edge of the blue. They had all the fauna of the sea to play with and ingenuity bred of boredom and absolute power.

Dodge understood now Elise's remark that there was inhuman cruelty abroad in the world and savored again and again the innuendo that had been there when she had promised that he would see. And he had been reeling like a woman-crazed adolescent on his first date. It made him sick. But, under the sea, you can't afford to be sick. You can't breathe and vomit at the same time—with only your mouth to fulfill both functions.

Of course, he'd tried to escape. After they had dragged

him back from his first escapade, he had tried again in exactly the same way, and this time they had sport before they sent him back to the algae beds. After the third attempt they moved him down to the deeper levels, and set him to tending fish, caged in wire mesh, under constant surveillance from guard towers.

And still he had tried. He'd nearly lost his life that time. They'd some way of controlling fish that was at once repellant and fascinating. He had been ringed by six-foot sharks—quite small and harmless, although he hadn't known that at the time—who circled him watchfully, like fishy mandogs, until they came for him.

It was then that he'd met Harp.

He'd been jettisoned into the sea once more, his wounds laved by the salt-water womb of mankind, and had gone flapping off to his stone niche in an air-bubble, feeling that he would never escape from this torment. The only thing that lived in him was his hatred for Elise. It was only that that prevented his madness from taking another turn, a turn from which he would never have recovered. Another sadly-limping slave of the underseas flew past him, then curved painfully back, fell in, and they finned together back to the rest bubble. Inside, breathing air through nose as well as mouth and stretching cramped limbs, Dodge saw that his companion was short and broad. That was the first thing you noticed about him, his squareness. Then you saw his square jaw, square nose and strangely light-colored eyes that had a habit of widening suddenly as though in perpetual surprise at the world. There were cruel wounds on his back, like those on Dodge's, and he had no need to ask many questions.

"How'd you get off?"

Dodge laughed shortly, an ugly bark of sound.

"I waited until they were bringing in a fresh lot of sardines and flew out against the stream. Sharks," he finished succinctly. To the underseas slaves, all fish that were not carnivores were sardines.

The man nodded. "I'm Harp. Call me that because I used to be handy with a harpoon."

"Used to be?"

"Haven't handled one in what must be years. At least,

44

it seems like it." Dodge knew what he meant. The stars—
to see the stars, just once again . . .

They'd fallen to talking, and Dodge found that Harp,
too, shared a deep and bitter resentment against his kid-
nappers. He whistled when Dodge mentioned that he'd
been taken off the Blue Deep Hotel.

"They're getting too insolent." He shifted his naked
thighs on the stone. Dodge perceived the incongruity between position and remark; in it he found nothing humorous. "They'll be flying up the Thames and snatching
members from the Terrace soon," Harp finished morosely.

"I think mine was a special case."

"Oh?"

"What did you do before . . ." Dodge changed the subject.

Harp smiled crookedly. "Underwater flying instructor.
Ironic isn't it? Out on a little deep-sea instruction, and up
pops a sub, snatches me, class and all." His voice was bitter. "I should have known better. Me, Harp, being press-
ganged right into my own element. Sucker."

"I'd no idea this went on . . ."

"Not many people do, there lies the tragedy and the
strength of the system. Oh, it's a system, all right. The
Bishop Wilkins Corps have all the answers taped. You recall we were stuffed into a sub-tow balloon a while back
and stifled in there for six hours? That was the U.O.P."

"U.O.P.?"

"Under Ocean Patrol. They're the supervising body for
all underwater development. Had a pal with them once.
Pierre thought he'd go his way, I'd go mine. I don't suppose he's rotting in an undersea tomb like this now."

"You mean an inspection was on?"

"Right. If we could make a break from that balloon
next time round . . ."

That had been the beginning of a friendship that had
outlasted many moments of mutual danger. But they'd
played it carefully; steal a scrap of steel here, snatch a
loose screw there. Hoard air-tanks that were ostensibly
empty and return them in reverse order when they were
changed, so that gradually they built up a store of fully-
charged tanks. Try to get two of the new facepieces. That
had been impossible.

"Refraction index of water is different from that of air," Harp said once. "That's why you can't see much under with naked eyes, apart from the salt. And ordinary glass goggles and facemasks give you an impression that everything is a third larger than it really is. That's the refraction index being changed in the plane of glass between air and water. These high-class masks have vision corrected facepieces." But they hadn't secured any, and had, perforce, to make do with the old.

Harp warned Dodge that not all the sudden activity which flurried the farm was caused by raids of the U.O.P. They were working around a group of clumsy underwater barges, bringing fresh soil from the land to create further areas of controlled cultivation, and extend man's aquiculture deeper into the sea, when they were swept up and thrust into the stuffiness of a sub-tow balloon.

Inside, the rumors went round.

"Big raid by another Bishop Wilkins mob. Saw tiger sharks attacking—manta rays and riders—harpoons—antipersonnel depth charges—cut to pieces . . ."

Dodge looked at Harp.

"We don't escape from this lot only to be swept up by another just as bad. Sweat it out. This internecine warfare goes on all the time. 'Recruits for the working staff,' they probably call it." Harp licked his lips. "This life we can take—just. We might jump straight out into something a long sight worse."

When the excitement died down and the slaves went back to work, Dodge and Harp felt they had been spared to escape another day. They began working hard, became model laborers, threw off the suspicion engendered by their earlier attempts to escape. Their hoarding of air tanks, both helium and oxygen, went on.

Events had moved swiftly for them then. They'd had their first real slice of luck when they'd been assigned to the sprats' cages—sprats being baby sardines—for nursery work. Sprats had to be hand-fed vitamin-rich food in a carefully controlled explosion of growth, so that they could be rapidly converted into mature animals; that entailed almost individual feeding, usually carried out in quarter-mile-wide cages only a few feet below the surface. It was a boring, monotonous job—but then, all jobs were monotonous in the blue monotony of the underseas—and they'd had time, snatched in furtive half minutes, to cut out a section of wire and plan how they would bend it back at the moment of escape.

And that moment was almost here.

Down below, cruising subs distributed food, allowing it to fall freely through the superimposed layers of cages; up here it had to be processed in the tanks moored on their cables around the edges of the cage. The black bulk of one loomed up now, with the agile figures of workers around it; then the pinging signal ceased, all the sprats fluttered like a darting cloud of birds, all in the same instant, all turning with a flash of silver, and came sweeping back like wind-driven leaves.

The electric currents affecting the fish's spinal cords had no power over men, but Dodge had the usual feeling that it was easier to turn and fly back the way he had come. He did so. But this time he felt a mounting excitement in him. This time would be the last. This time they would not respond to the warning ping from the far tower.

CHAPTER FIVE

When the opposite haze of wire loomed up at them from the limpid water, they had angled off sufficiently to be out of sight of the control tower. Beyond their undulating flippers the swarming cloud of sprats advanced, like smoke rolling over downland. Ahead, the wire.

Harp suddenly raced forward, his fins pumping, his hands outstretched. In a matter of moments he had found the pre-cut opening and was bending back the tough wire. Dodge flew up and helped. He could hear Harp's grunts of effort. Bubbles rose, expanding, and burst above. The ceiling was quite near, a shimmering chiaroscuro of mercury and ebony. The sun must be quite low now. The wire gave. They slipped through.

Their first action was to jettison the fish-food packs, after withdrawing the spare air-tanks concealed in them.

They had no idea in the world where they were; they might have been in Chinese or Australian or Caribbean waters; all they knew for certain was that they were near the tropical seas of food in plenty. They flew forward, fast but cautiously.

This time they'd make it! This time they could not fail. They'd both eaten well at the prescribed time before emerging from their bubble to go on shift; the extra vitamins and sugar and fatty foods, part of all undersea diet, would give them a long immunity to the extra conductivity of the water draining off their body heat. After that; hunt for fishy food. They'd live, of that Dodge felt supremely confident.

He was checking his water bottle when the first shapes flitted through the water towards them. He knew at once that these sharks were the watchdogs, harmless unless roused by the scent of blood or the sounds of a dying fish, and they'd planned to push on through them, unmindful of their sharp noises herding them into the center of a narrowing circle.

Harp thrust forward confidently. Dodge, bolstering his courage, followed. The sharks, puzzled, fell in behind. Whatever eerie control was exercised over them, they could not think coherently like a man, and Dodge was conscious of a wave of triumph, of contempt, for the killers. The procession flew through the depths.

Dodge saw Harp gesture. He flew alongside. The harpooner pointed, his facemask showing his eyes, large and round. Dodge looked.

Bulking like a whale the flank of a sub-tow balloon drifted slowly towards them. Finned fingers boiled around it. Slaves, being herded through the airlocks. Dodge surmised wildly that the U.O.P. must be making a snap inspection, and all slaves were being rounded up. This had fouled up their plans. Unless they could slip away unseen they stood no chance against the weapons of the overseers.

"*Let there be no panic,*" Dodge thought, unconsciously repeating an old motto. He sprang with a single powerful lunge of his flippers, followed Harp away from the menace of the balloon. It dropped back into the bluish obscurity.

The water was like soup. Steadily, darkness increased. In front, like beckoning will o' the wisps, tiny lights began to glow, throwing erratic streaks of radiance through the waters. The lights approached. Harp moved his arm; they struck off towards one side. More lights glowed. Harp threw a quick glance over his shoulder, assured himself that Dodge was closed up, and dived. They flew down, feeling the coldness seeping into their flesh, trying to circumvent the onrushing lights.

The sensation was like trying to reach the moon at the bottom of a well. They descended for what seemed ages and still the lights paced them. Dodge knew what they were, all right. Hunting beasts. Phosphorescent or electric-powered lights strapped to the backs of sharp, fast fish, with ultrasonic transmitters and echo-sounders, spreading out to detect and report any movement beneath the seas. The Bishop Wilkins Corporations was expecting company, all right.

And Dodge and Harp had got themselves caught on the inside of the barrier. Angry, futile resentment burned in Dodge. All their scheming, all their planning, to come to naught because their so-called saviors had chosen this very moment to carry out another abortive inspection.

Presently Harp touched Dodge. He shook his head, pointed up. They were as deep as they dared dive with their equipment; they had to rise. Fuming, impotent, they soared upwards, retreating always before the cold hostility of the lights.

In the balloon, Dodge thought. *Maybe that's our best chance.*

He gestured to Harp—the incommunicability of under-sea life always filled him with a wrenching sense of in-completeness, of foetal helplessness. He shaped with his hands, pointed back, shrugged his shoulders.

Harp caught on.

Tiredly, they flew back towards the balloon. There was always the chance they might run into the U.O.P. patrol. Before they reached the balloon the sentinel sharks caught up with them again, sniffed around, and then, because the men were going the right way, left them for other duties. Harp and Dodge ploughed on. Radiance grew in the sea. Flippered foremen flew here and there, harpoons bristling, contagious in their excitement. A free shoal of fish gy-rated crazily across their field of vision. A sub prowled below, its wash forcing them upwards, throwing them too close to the watchful overseers.

Too quickly for Dodge to follow, they were included in a frightened batch of slaves, hustled towards the bal-loon. Its sheet metal sides gleamed in the green lighting, black airlocks gaped. They went through. Standing awk-wardly on the gratings, with the valves closing, Dodge thought: *"This is the end. We'll never get away now."* He wished, savagely, that they had thrust through the watchful ring of guardians—then knew at once that the only result of that would have been death. Immediate, unpleasant death at the fangs of the outer guardians, triggered by the impulses from the guardian fish and their electronic relays.

Lights blazed down outside the locks as the valves closed slowly. Into that haze of brilliance Dodge saw men rising from the deeps. Men who wore narrow, curved facemasks, men who had no breathing equipment—men who breathed water.

His breath caught raggedly in his throat.

He stared, fascinated. They swarmed upwards, forming a chain, and the manacles on their wrists and the short lengths of steel wire that joined their legs gleamed, as links of fire between the human links of flesh. Men, breathing water!

Their faces were dull, sagging. They moved sluggishly, foolishly, almost, with dazed uncaring motions that jerked them cruelly against the tethers.

The lock valves closed. Water began to run from the gratings.

Dodge turned to Harp, ripping his mouthpiece out as soon as the water dropped below his chin.

"Those men. Breathing water! Was I dreaming?"

Harp's eyes blazed the self-same queries.

A dry, mirthless chuckle sounded. They whirled.

A bent, withered, dried-up oldster, in the full meaning of that term in undersea life, was looking at them derisively. His green eyes gleamed madly. Others in the lock were clustering round. Questions spurted from them like undersea volcanoes. The oldster chuckled again and silenced the babble immediately.

"Menfish! They've been at work again. Catastrophe and destruction. I see it."

Dodge brushed aside the thought that the old man was over-acting; he was much too excited. Harp shook the thin shoulders savagely.

"Who were they, pop? Do you know?"

"Menfish. Men, breathing water, like fish. They get—made over—like that."

It was betrayingly warm in the lock. Smell was coming back into the world as the men removed their masks.

Smell of warm rubber, and fishy, salty odor of bleached bodies, oil from mechanisms—Dodge stared at the old man.

"Who makes them over?"

"The Wilkins Corps, who else?" The old man's face was lined with the worries of years. He must have been under-ocean for quite a while. He knew about menfish—no one else seemed to. Harp asked a sharp question. The oldster chuckled. "Use 'em out on the precipice. Deep. They can fly down a thousand feet or more."

"I just don't believe it," Dodge breathed. And yet he had to. Because now he knew he hadn't been dreaming when he'd had that split-second vision of the men breathing water, when Elise Tarrant had laughed and goaded them on.

"You'll all end up like that." The oldster's voice wheezed. "I wasn't tough enough; but you'll all get changed. Turned into fish."

On that shrill, amused cackle in the dotard's voice, the inner valves opened and they all spewed out into the sub-tow balloon. Dodge climbed mechanically, clawing his way up the interminable ladders and edging out along the latticework of girders, like a chicken battery, until he and Harp wedged themselves into a cross-piece corner. Harp had a good grip on the oldster's shoulder.

"Now, pop," he began seriously. "Tell us all about these menfish."

"Nothing to say, son." The cracked voice was sane now, sane and level, and filled with a fullness startling to Dodge. "Name's Eli, son. Wait." Eli put his hand to his mouth, gave a convulsive jerk, and then beamed at them in the full glory of a full set of plastics. "Daren't wear me teeth flying, might lose me mouthpiece. Got a special grip."

"What do you mean, nothing to say?" Dodge said impatiently. Around them the balloon was filling with the frightened whimper of cowed slaves, and Dodge caught faintly the shrill scream as women were herded in.

"The Wilkins Corps who farm out near the edge use menfish. Have to. Depth. Once they finish that surgical treatment on you—son, you stay in the sea for the rest of your life."

"You mean—you can't breathe air?"

"Precisely."

Eli shifted around on the metal slats. He was wearing a water-soaked singlet which left his arms free, and even though some of the slaves who bothered with clothing had removed it and were attempting to dry it, with little success, Eli seemed to hug his singlet all the more closely to him. There were bulges beneath, showing clearly through the clinging wet material.

"Menfish," said Harp, dazed. "Under the water for the rest of your life. My God, Jerry—someone ought to do something about all this."

"What?" Old Eli said grimly. He was not so old, nor so decrepit, they saw now. "The government is powerless beyond the immediate area of their undersea forts. Like now, by the time a patrol is anywhere near, the watcher fish with Asdic have them spotted, the slaves are rounded up. Easy enough to lose a sub-tow balloon down under." He stretched. "Me for some food. There, round the fires."

Electric fires were burning on low power and the slaves clustered round, shivering, steaming. Food was passed around. Time passed. Noises had an odd effect in the sound-distorting helium atmosphere; of diminishing in the vast balloon, and then returning in a crescendoing circle. Dodge was thinking of the menfish and of escaping. A tension built up in him, so that his hands were all a-tremble. He felt very alone.

"We've got to get away, Harp," he said desperately. "We can't have that happen to us."

Screams and cries floated up to them. Harp put his head over the edge of the metal slat, stared down. His body tensed. Dodge shoved his head out and looked down.

Overseers, not brutal, just callous and beyond further understanding of human suffering, were herding a huddled group of women along the dizzying latice of metal slats. One fell to her knees and a woman bent quickly and helped her to her feet. Dodge stared, a sick, hot, choking feeling boiling into his stomach and throat, making his eyes blur.

The girl standing proudly erect down there had three scraps of defiant scarlet attached to her naked body. She had weals across her back. She was a slave.

Elise Tarrant was a slave, just like Dodge.

Then—she hadn't engineered his kidnapping?

He leaned over to shout to her and her face lifted, met his. No expression marred the blank beauty of that icy mask. She stared, for a long moment their eyes clung, then she turned away, stumbling off with the others. Dodge realized that he was gripping the metal slat so tightly his hands were numb. Elise Tarrant a slave. *Elise.*

He said: "I'm getting out of here, Harp. Now. I'm taking that girl. Coming?"

CHAPTER SIX

Roland Benedek, Lieutenant, U.O.P., was an embittered man. He pushed his tall conical casque up, automatically opening the slats, and stared narrow-eyed as the sub-tow balloon disappeared into the dim blue distance. No hope of catching that. His seven-man patrol closed up. They knew, as well as he, the futility of all this. The veering shadow of a sub moved across their field of vision, spotted them and sheered away. No markings, of course. This Barny McCracken Wilkins Corps was clever—he could have sworn he'd seen men—slaves—being bundled into the balloon. The camera would tell if they had, but that wasn't evidence; the corp would counter with: "Just workers, that's all." He pulled his mouthpiece free and spat. Then he replaced the tube and called base on the ultra-sound set.

Report—nil.

The submarine that Benedek had seen prowled on. She closed the wallowing sub-tow balloon fast, her asdic vectoring her up with the precision of a turret-lathe. Now, thought Danny Agostini, now was the best time of all. The same thrill shot through him; hunting fish was a sport —hi-jacking men was something indescribable. He pulled his lower lip down, unconsciously strengthening his weasel look, his pointed nose almost quivering at the target ahead.

"Hold her," he said unpleasantly to the helmsmen.

The sub was on railway tracks. The forward screen

55

showed the nearing flank of the balloon, studded with airlocks. It was like puncturing a boil—almost. The thought of ramming into that putrescent sausage, spilling out screaming people—screaming in water—filled Agostini with an indescribable glee. But the boss wouldn't like it. Men were needed—his lower lip sucked in behind the yellow, uneven teeth.

An airlock was opening. Figures slid through, flippers blurring as they shot away in a steep dive. Sport!

Agostini leant forward eagerly, gave explicit directions. The submarine rushed down, like a huge gray sea-wolf, on the flying mites of humans. Agostini quite failed to see the second sub swinging round to bring him directly into her sights.

The balloon was filled with the sigh and murmur of hundreds of people perched, damp and uncomfortable, on the lattice work of metal girders. The air was foul. Condensation splashed everywhere. Some slaves, weaker than others, were breathing from their air-tanks, reckless of the consequences.

Harp said slowly: "All right, Jerry. I'm with you."

Dodge nodded confidently. He jerked his head down. They went down the ladder swiftly, moving with crabbed ease in air, dropped to the gangway. Dodge ran lightly in the direction taken by Elise and other women. He found them lying exhausted on bare metal, their limp bodies as bare and sexlessly uninteresting as the steel.

"All right, Romeo. That's far enough."

The guard, his bare chest a mat of heavy hair, stepped forward arrogantly. He lifted the short-barreled undersea harpoon gun. That thing could disembowel in air.

Dodge hit him once, quite scientifically, surprised that the pure hate foaming in his mind allowed of competent level action. He did kick the fellow as he went down, though, and that surprised him in its sheer uncharacteristic bombshell-like quality. It showed what was happening to his mind.

"We've little chance as it is," he said in a detached tone. "We can only take Elise—there." He pointed, and Harp swivelled to look.

Elise's face still wore that mask of chiselled horror. She stared at Dodge as though he were a tree. He took her arm, unconscious of the way his fingers bit into her biceps. A slim, tigrish figure uncoiled from the mass of apathetic women, launched itself at Dodge.

Harp shuffled forward, caught the squirming body of the girl who breathed quick hissing spurts of hatred at him, lifting her sweet, heart-shaped face in blind panic.

"Hold it, sister," rumbled Harp. "I'm not gonna hurt you."

Dazedly, Dodge recognized the Siamese girl who had tumbled off the aquaplane—oh, years ago.

Elise said: "Stop it, Lura. We can't do anything."

"All right." Dodge notched off another chance of escaping. "We'll take your girl friend. Harp can look after her."

"Hey . . ." Harp said.

Dodge silenced him with a quick, impatient cut of his hand. He hauled Elise after him along the gangway, saw that Harp, after an explosive monosyllable, was following with the girl, who was disdainfully shaking off Harp's big fingers. Harp had the harpoon gun and that was quite obviously far more important to him than the indignant Siamese girl. From some impossible well of strength deep within him, Dodge drew a smile of amusement; it lasted a bare half-second, frightening him with its incongruity. Perhaps, Elise . . .

There was no trouble reaching the air lock by which they had entered the balloon, and Dodge had a flicker of hope riding him until the three guards came running, their *totschläger* swinging up on cords to smack into their palms. The four slaves had their plastic flippers slung on a cord round their necks, standard procedure when walking in air spaces, and the movement of Harp's harpoon gun must have been partially masked by his flippers, hanging over his chest.

He fired three times. The Siamese girl's face went gray and her mouth opened. Dodge cut the scream off. Elise's expression had not changed. Dodge wasn't feeling too steady around the gills, either. The valves opened and they moved forward. Elise said: "I'm sorry, Commander. It's all my fault. Mr. Grosvenor . . ." Her face was pleading with him. Then it went stiff. She said, sharply: "Commander! Guard . . ."

Dodge whirled. Elise's voice was amputated by a flat crack, magnified into booming echoes in the metal box, wildly distorted by the helium-oxygen atmosphere of the balloon. A guard who had run up and leveled his harpoon gun sagged at the knees, a shocked look of surprise on his face. Blood stained his uniform tunic. Without thinking, Dodge hurled the others into the lock, thumbed the valves closed. The lock cycled water as they adjusted their undersea equipment. Even then, no one said anything.

Who had fired the shot killing the guard who had them dead in the sights of his harpoon gun?

He was still mulling that over in his mind as the outer valves opened and they thrust forward, flippers blurring with speed, heading out and away from the macabre microcosm in the world of the undersea.

They saw the stalking shadow when it was far too late. From the side of the sub, under Agostini's personal gloating direction, a filament net jutted. The cloud of hair-fine wires exploded, formed a net, circled and englobed the flyers. Dodge tried to rip the net-strands—once.

After that, he relaxed, or tried to, despair and anger and self-contempt and blazing hatred for this murky watery life of the deepsea eating his vitals. Space . . .

They were hauled in, squirming and struggling, trying to prevent themselves from being squashed against each other. For a single pitiful second Dodge had the flaring hope that this was a U.O.P. ship. Then sanity caught up with him and he recognized that there was no hope for him—or his comrades—now. The lock of the submarine led to a decompression chamber; they had to be staged down to one atmosphere carefully, helium or no helium, after their long immersion in the deep waters and the compensated pressure of the balloon. It was going to be a long process, making sure the bubbles came out of their blood and sinew quietly, without fuss and the crippling bends.

Without quite realizing how it had happened, Dodge and Harp were alone in a partitioned recompression chamber. Elise and her Siamese friend had vanished behind metal walls.

He was exhausted and desperately hungry. Undersea life demanded enormous quantities of vitamins and sugars;

his skin was white and puckered, like the dead belly of a shark. Looking at things dispassionately, Dodge came to grips with the knowledge that he had made a hash of everything—and tried to lie to himself, to tell himself that even now he would come out all right—with Elise.

In his mind it rang hollow, like the infuriatingly insane laughter of a hyena.

Some twenty-five feet forward and above him, in the control room, Danny Agostini drove his sub headlong towards the bloated balloon. His warped mind sang with excitement, a drool of saliva escaped from the corner of his mouth. And then the asdic lookout screamed a warning, Agostini took the situation in at a glance, his weasel brain answered the problem quicker than a nuclear-reaction, and the sub veered, almost waggled her hips away from the path of the torpedoes. They drummed off somewhere astern, trimmed and armed, heading out into the blue. The other sub swung her bows, lining up a fresh shot

Agostini made his decision, cursed the luck that had stolen a fat, slave-filled balloon from under his eyes by the intervention of a guarding sub, and sent his vessel burrowing through the water back to his base. The boss could be very rough on an inefficient sub captain, and even rougher on Agostini, his personal executioner.

The sub crashed through three fish pens, trailing weed-streaming nets from her emergency schnorkel gear until the net-cutters sawed through. Then Agostini chanced using an open-water lane and settled down to cruising speeds. He had had the idea that one of his captives had been a woman—life might be interesting, yet. He decided to find out.

Dodge did not know of the men who came for Elise and Lura. He heard sharp sounds through the metal partition, and guessed that pressure must be down to about one atmosphere now. The sub's maneuverings he had taken and forgotten. He could not feel anything about the future, anything at all.

Harp sat crouched on the damp metal, cold and hungry and miserable.

"I might have known getting that harpoon was too good to last," he mumbled through shivering lips.

"What's happened to us?" Dodge asked without great interest.

"Just another Bishop Wilkins Corp. They fight each other all the time. Hi-jacking. God, I'm hungry!"

Dodge felt too dispirited to answer. When at last high calorific food and sugar-lumps were brought by close-mouthed crewmen he ate ravenously, his questions unanswered; and then they were hustled along to a cramped metal-walled space that contained just three inflated mattresses. They were asleep before the guards had locked the doors. Their natural sleep passed into a drugged coma as the gas flooded silently and invisibly into the cell.

Back in U.O.P. Base Trident, Simon Hardy was reading Lieutenant Benedek's report, too disillusioned to curse.

At UN Headquarters, Secretary Henderson was girding his loins to outsmart Toxter at the coming fiscal enquiry.

A certain Mr. Grosvenor was an extremely worried man.

And, under the Moon's scoured surface, a group of high ranking Space Force officers were deciding upon a course of action.

Dodge, when he was taken through into the undersea world of domes and caves perched on the edge of the escarpment, knew nothing of those moves in the wider world. His first awareness of himself was awakening to a pattern of pain filamenting his body. His throat hurt. He breathed deeply, trying to clear the kelp clogging his brain. He was not wearing a facemask or air cylinders.

He was lying on a rough mattress that felt as though it had been stuffed with coral, with stone walls surrounding him on three sides and a metal wall on the fourth. The walls and floor were completely bare. A light fixture was embedded in heavy glass in the center of the ceiling. A grating, high up on the door, was barred with inch thick steel rods.

Raising his hand to his aching head was an effort requiring immense concentration. For a long moment he did not know what had happened, where he was—he had an insane idea that his spaceship had been petrified—or what he was doing. He stared dazedly at the grating.

Something came through the grating that told him everything he wanted to know—everything—and more.

It told him that he was doomed. It told him that he must fight if he wanted to preserve his sanity—and he wasn't sure that he wanted to remain sane. It was a simple, pleasant little thing.

It was a fish that swam lazily in through the grating of his room.

CHAPTER SEVEN

Ocean Secretary Henderson and Minister of Aquiculture George Werner were in the midst of a deeply distressing conference when the deep-sea call came in from Admiral Simon Hardy of the Under Ocean Patrol. The screen lit up, showing at once the grim-faced, teak-jawed admiral, the stump of his left arm jerking irritably at his side. Seeing was good, the ultra-sonics carrying both vision and sound clearly from the depths of the sea, six hundred feet down.

"I've just received your call, Henderson. Had an Urgent in from a patrol."

"Hullo, Simon," Henderson said, hoping that the atmosphere would be allowed to settle before he had to say what he had to say. Simon Hardy was a crusty old shellback at the best of times. "Hear that you lost another sub in the Juliana Trench."

"Don't worry, Henderson. I didn't disobey orders. The sub was on patrol and this happened before the recall went out." Hardy was obviously suffering under a load of repressed emotion that was threatening to blow his skull apart.

"I didn't think you had, Simon. After Sub Nine was dragged down, I don't think even an old fire-eater like you would send another one into that area without some very deep thinking."

It was a sore subject with both men; the Minister of

62

Aquiculture shifted uneasily and then a short-lived smile of relief flitted over his face as they decided to drop that conversation and switch the subject to less explosive channels.

"I've been thinking I ought to drop out and visit you at Trident, Simon," Henderson said.

"Surely. Surely." Hardy betrayed nothing, yet there was warmth in his tone. These men had been the pioneers of aquiculture, forcing through their crash programs of undersea farming and production, pitch-forking new ideas into the maelstrom of discontent and hunger engulfing the Earth, until at last something had given way. That something had been hide-bound authority. Now the continental plains ringing the sea-coasts were a-swarm with the Bishop Wilkins Corporations. More food was grown under the sea than above it. Processed fish and fish-products were on every table—and few housewives could be certain that what they were cooking had once had the unmistakable tang of fish. It had been a Piscean revolution.

Hardy's blunt-fingered hand caressed his chin, then dropped to the stump of his left arm. He gripped the piece of elbow that was left. There was a faraway look in his eyes. Henderson, watching, knew what Hardy was thinking.

"Was it all worth it, Simon?" he asked softly.

Hardy opened his eyes to stare straight from the screen at the Ocean Secretary. "Worth it! Every damned minute of it—including this!" And he brandished the stump. "I'm not a dry-neck, never could be, now." He puffed out his lips. "How do you stand it there, Henderson, stranded on dry land at UN Headquarters? Don't you ever get sick for the sea again?"

"I'm coming to visit you, Simon," Henderson reminded.

"Sure." Hardy nodded his head to the Minister of Aquiculture. "Bring George, too. Both of you could stand getting real wet all over."

Werner and Henderson smiled, a little shamefacedly, a little placatingly. Old Hardy was more than a fanatic on deep-sea life—they almost believed that if there were no Admiral Simon Hardy, there would be no undersea life.

Werner said: "I'd like that, Simon."

Beyond the open window—which did nothing for the

laboring air-conditioning plant—the parks and lawns and shade trees stretched away towards the city outline, stabbing the horizon like a jagged, paling fence. The afternoon air was filled with the muted hum of millions of people, all busy, all preoccupied with life and its problems, all enjoying to the full the benefits culled by science from the waters of the oceans of the world. Thinking that, all three men—Henderson and Werner in the UN skyscraper, Hardy in his submarine rockwalled fortress—could at least grasp at the illusion that they had done something worthwhile with their lives. At the very least, they had staved off the starvation that lowered over the world before the seas had been opened up.

The harsh jangle of his intercom broke into that quiet, meditative pause, and Henderson sighed and opened the key.

"Captain Pinhorn, Space Force to see you sir."

"Send him in."

Henderson, flipping off the intercom, said over his shoulder so that Hardy could hear: "We were talking about this Captain Pinhorn when you called, Simon." The atmosphere of tension was back.

"Anything to do with me?"

"Unfortunately, yes. He's come down from the Moon on the trail of a Space Force officer who has disappeared." Henderson's thin face showed resigned disapproval. "Claims he was kidnapped underwater."

"I don't think any Bishop Wilkins Corporation would be crazy enough to pressgang a serving Space Force Officer. What are the details?"

In the brief moment before the door opened and the announcement of Captain Pinhorn, Henderson had ample time to say: "Fellow went to the Blue Deep Hotel—you remember it, Simon—with a girl working for his uncle's manager. Uncle just died or something. All we know for sure is that both of them disappeared there; they didn't come back. Checked in at the Blue Deep, went for a hunt —and vanished." Henderson painted a genial smile across his nervous features. "Ah, Captain Pinhorn, come in! Sit down. Cigarette?"

"How-de-do, sir. No thanks, don't smoke."

"Good. Under Ocean and Space have that in common, anyway, Captain."

Pinhorn sat down, flicking his Space Force blacks into their leading-edge crease in the gesture that every Space Force officer must have had ingrained into him at Academy. His body was small and compact, his head set well back on his neck so that he had always the impression of arrogantly challenging all the world. His thin black moustache and dark skin followed that pattern of aggressiveness. His soft speech was the outer mark of an iron self-restraint that existed only because its owner was firmly convinced that he was not just as good as the next man, but a good few parsecs better.

Pinhorn, without preamble, said: "Thank you for seeing me so quickly, sir. I'd like to get on this thing right away. I'm not allowed to tell you the full details, but Commander Dodge is required urgently for a special assignment."

Henderson decided to show his teeth, too.

"Saturn?"

Pinhorn did not betray by a single muscle that he was either dismayed, displeased or bored. He was a singularly self-contained man, withdrawn from the world in which lay his work—the world lying below the normal paths of men's minds and actions.

"Commander Dodge went to his hotel with a Miss Tarrant, that I found out from the hotel in town he'd left as his leave address. He had mentioned to friends that his uncle had died, and that he was needed on Earth to clear matters up. When the nature of those matters came to my attention, I immediately contacted you as the Head of Under Ocean.'

Down in his fortress under the sea, Hardy was wondering just why Henderson had bothered with all this personally. Henderson's normal method would be to initial an aide's report.

Then Pinhorn said: "Commander Dodge's uncle is—or was—Arthur Dodge, who, you may know . . ."

Simon Hardy burst out, startling the others: "The Artful Dodger! So he's dead, is he? I hadn't heard."

Captain Pinhorn swivelled to stare at the screen. His eyes and eyebrows asked questions. Henderson, looking on, felt a wry amusement. Certainly old Simon Hardy looked like nothing on Earth, with his naked torso, bulging eyes from the contact lenses, hair waving about when he moved and settling into that familiar white helmet when he was still, and irritably jerking a stump of arm that seldom ever was still—and that was true, anyway. Hardy wasn't on the Earth, he was under the sea. And Pinhorn, not recognizing him, merely underlined the gulf between Space and Under Ocean. An aching gulf that no one seemed bothered about bridging. Henderson said: "Captain Pinhorn, Space Force; Admiral Hardy, U.O.P."

And luxuriated in his satisfaction as Pinhorn took it.

The spaceman's recovery was good. He went on evenly talking. "I cannot contact the manager, a Mr. Grosvenor, and the affairs of the Arthur Dodge Bishop Wilkins Corporation are in an uproar. So I came to the top." He paused, and then said: "Tell me, sir. Why are all the undersea farm companies called Bishop Wilkins Corporations?"

"I thought everyone knew that. When Admiral Hardy, Mr. Werner, the Minister of Aquiculture, and myself began the work which was to lead up to the undersea situation we have today, we decided, to avoid complications, that it would be fair to dub our brainchildren with the name of the man who had first conceived the idea. The earliest man we knew of was Bishop Wilkins." He turned his head. "How does it go, Simon?"

Simon Hardy smiled, as though thinking back on days that had been very good.

"Bishop Wilkins lived back about the seventeenth century and was enthusiastic about diving and submarines and the new underwater toys that the Renaissance had thrown up again after fifteen hundred years' desuetude. They had some weird equipment in those days! Anyway, as far as we can tell, Wilkins was the first man actually to commit to print ideas for a real undersea colony, with air chambers and corridors, and divers living and working down there." He quirked his lips. "Perhaps I should say here, he saw a real and vivid picture, did that ancient visionary."

Pinhorn said as levelly as he could: "Did he also foresee the possibility that the owners of the undersea colonies would pressgang people to work? That they'd use methods abhorrent even to his days?" He put one fist on top of the other and pressed hard. "A commander of the Space Force has been kidnapped to work undersea—a victim of outdated and barbarous methods of labor recruitment. I know my superiors don't like the idea at all: I don't— and I feel confident that while this practice continues you gentlemen cannot feel that all is well with Under Ocean."

It was hard. There sounded the knights in shining armor. The gulf between those who lived on and above the surface, and those who passed their days under the sea, was a gulf of ideology so profound that three generations had done nothing to fill a fraction of it. For a vertiginous moment Henderson had to hold back his anger. How dare these puritans, who eagerly ate the food produced by undersea, so loftily condemn them out of hand!

"All right, gentlemen," he said at last. "We deplore the disappearance of Commander Dodge, Captain. I must say personally, that as you appear to have a knowledge of the pressgang system used by some Corporations, I can only suggest that no Wilkins Corporation is going to be fool enough to kidnap a Space Force Officer." He held up a hand as Pinhorn tried to interrupt. "However, as you seem convinced that your man has been kidnapped, I put it to you that you won't see him again."

It was blunt, brutal—but it was the only way.

"As you know, sir," Pinhorn said, "I am an Intelligence officer of the Space Force. My duty is to find Commander Dodge. I intend to do that—with or without your help."

Henderson raised his shoulders. "Very well. Then the best thing you can do is come out with us to Trident. That's Admiral Hardy's base. You might find something there to make you change your mind."

"I doubt it, sir. But I'll be in the sea. And that's where I have to be if I'm to find Jerry Dodge."

CHAPTER EIGHT

You're walking quietly along the street one day and you fall down an open manhole.

That's bad.

You're out of luck that day, all right. You look around, more annoyed at being such an idiot than frightened or hurt.

And then you realize that you've dropped into Dante's Inferno. Deeper than you thought. And the realization sinks in—and sinks in—and you'll never get out, never, never, never . . .

You'll breathe water the rest of your life.

You're a manfish—you'll never breathe air again.

Under the sea, for ever . . .

Commander Jeremy Dodge, Space Force, remained insane for a period of time that for ever afterwards was a blank, nightmare-peopled hiatus in his life. His last conscious mental picture was of a fish, idly swimming through the bars of his cell. His next impression, that was not distorted by the madness rotting in his brain, was of the same fish, or a relation, idly swimming back through the cell grating.

He lay, eyes open, for a long while, staring at nothing. This was his moment of truth—this was where he came face to face with the complete knowledge of himself. Whether he could square up to what his life was to be, accept it, not merely rationalize it out—that way had

caused too many psychotics before now—but come to terms with it; see it for merely another facet of what he had to do, what he was born to do and be. Complete acceptance of life under the sea as part of his destiny was the only course that could bring him anything apart from pain and madness and death.

And—he didn't want to die.

He sat up on the bunk and spread his fingers and passed his hand before his eyes. He could feel the resistance of the water. But there was nothing to see that he would not have seen had he performed that action in air. He put a hand to his face. No face-mask. Yet he was convinced that he could see as perfectly as he could in air; and Harp had said that the refractive index of water made human eyes useless. His fumbling fingers found the answer. Contact lenses. Immersed always in salt water they could stay in permanently, without the burning irritation, that came in time, when worn in air.

How he relished that phrase: "In air!"

He was breathing in long natural rhythms that seemed perfectly ordinary, and there was a relaxed feeling of goodness in his throat. Salt water was the cradle of all life. A man's lung could be adapted, he supposed, or maybe they'd been cut clean out and gill cavities substituted; but then, his chest wouldn't rise and fall, would it? He shook his head. Acceptance, once it was accepted, brought other problems.

A curious droning, rising and falling, attracted his attention and he cocked an ear. It took him a few moments to sort out what he was hearing, and then the truth hit him in the face and sent him back on the bunk, fighting the last residue of hysteria.

Somewhere, a brass band was playing the Prelude to Act Three of "Lohengrin."

He listened to the strains, sorting them out, realizing that the water played its own tricks with acoustics. Sound travels four times as fast in water as it does in air; but some of the high notes were awfully shaky. The rum-te-tum-tum of the big brass instruments seemed to seep into his nerves.

Then the door opened.

He was back to reality at once. Back to himself. Back to the reason why he was here.

"All right, pal. Come on out."

Obediently, he stood up. The foreman who hung in the doorway, watching him alertly, looking like any other undersea foreman that Dodge had had dealings with. The only difference was that he, too, breathed water. The seven shot harpoon gun was trained casually towards Dodge and the man's flippers quivered faintly under the readiness-state of his nerves and muscles. He wouldn't be easily jumped.

"Come on, come on!" The gun jerked impatiently.

"I'm coming," Dodge said—or tried to. He mouthed the words, moving his tongue and lips; but nothing sounded from his mouth. He tried again, a sudden panic flooding him that he was dumb. He could feel the water moving in his mouth, not unpleasantly, but not a noise could he make.

The overseer vented a grunt of disgust. "You can't talk, slavey. Pressure's too great—have to fly up nearer the surface for that. And that's just what you ain't gonna do."

Dodge saw the man's microphone and amplifier then, and understood. Resignedly he stood up and began to walk towards the door. It was tough going.

"Fly, slavey, fly. I ain't got all day."

Dodge thrust downward with his leg muscles and shot towards the doorway. The foreman beat once with his flippers and surged backwards, reversed with masterly skill and hung, all quivering, the harpoon stabbing at Dodge's navel.

"That wasn't clever. Not clever at all. Just move around cautious-like. See?"

Dodge nodded dumbly. Beyond the foreman he could see other shapes in the rock-hewn passageway. Men, like himself breathing water, being roughly herded into line with quick blows of streamlined billies. So it was the same old story all over again. Without flippers it was harder to fly; but he made it and fell in with the other slaves.

There was no sign of Harp. In these strange and peril-ous surroundings Dodge missed his companion's quick readiness and matter-of-fact knowledge of undersea life. But—what would Harp know about the menfish? Perhaps he hadn't been operated on? Flying laboriously up the corridor and emerging into a sketchily illuminated area where mudfalls sluiced down from the sheer rock walls rising in a half circle above, he began to remember other things and people from the life now forever closed to him.

Elise.

The ache of not seeing space again, of being barred from taking his ship up on the clean fire of atomic jets to the remote chips of light in the sky, of fighting his way in life to some mistily perceived, yet yearned for goal, all that had become numbed, as though it were part of his childhood. But Elise . . . Finding her and then losing her, twice over, was a treacherous trick of fate, or at least a monument to his own stupidity. He shuffled into line with the other slaves, feet stirring the sandy bottom, and peered about for signs of his friends. He recognized no one.

He began to feel cold. The coldness spread from his chest, crawling out like the flow of glaciers to every part of his body. Around him the other slaves were glancing uneasily about, moving their arms and legs uncertainly, held by the fears—so easily ingrained—of the foremen and their weapons. No one of them would be likely to make a break; it was getting uncomfortably cold. Dodge tried to tell himself that these underwater bosses wouldn't carry out expensive operations on men, and then allow them to die of cold as soon as they were roused; but if he didn't warm up soon, with water drawing off his body heat at its rapid rate, then he and the others would be seriously injured, if they didn't die.

Perched on an outcrop of rock, a man clad in foam rubber dress stood lazily on his fins and watched them. There was something at once menacing and hateful about his easy arrogance as he stood there, smiling down on them. At last the tension snapped. A few ranks away from Dodge a huge shock-haired man leaped up into the water, his broad face ugly, his knobbly fists clenched. His mouth opened and closed and Dodge guessed he was shouting violently, and within him Dodge had a passionate desire to identify himself with all the pent-up frustration displayed by this rebel. Then, as though understanding the ineffectiveness of his oral movements, the big man wrapped his arms around himself and shook. As an imitation of a cold man it was first class.

At once there was response. Four guards streaked towards the protesting slavey, hustled him away. The others were rapidly shepherded back into the rocky hole. As soon as they were inside, Dodge began to feel warmer.

The water in the maze of passages in the rock was artificially heated, then. Worth remembering.

Passing the grumbling thunder of turbines circulating the heated water, they were brought out into a globe-shaped cavern, where the foam-dressed man flew negligently, to stand on a small dais at one end. He began to speak. At first Dodge paid little heed to what he was saying, wrapped in his own thoughts, but the substance of the lecture quickly drew his attention.

"An interesting experiment. It should convince all of you that any attempt to escape is fruitless. The temperature of the outside water is low, about eighteen degrees Centigrade, and you would all be breathing that water, it would be inside you, and you would stiffen into frozen corpses so fast if you tried to escape that we wouldn't even bother to hunt after you."

In his present miserable frame of mind, that, Dodge was prepared to believe. The warmly clad man went on: "You still have a slight positive buoyancy, because your lungs do not entirely fill with water, if they did you'd sink having no buoyancy chamber, and the system adopted by our surgeons is the best available. You should feel honored." He was really enjoying this, Dodge noticed sourly. "You have observed the gill slits under your arms . . ."

Dodge nearly cricked his neck, twisting and turning, as did most of those about him. He couldn't quite see round far enough. Then he saw the man in front. There were a number of slits under the arms, running between his ribs, and as Dodge watched, horrified, they opened lazily, and then, just as lazily, closed. He felt round with a trembling finger and his hand recoiled as it encountered the slits in his own body.

"You take in water through your nose and mouth, and your glottal stop is, by this time, reacting automatically. The human organism reacts wonderfully well, the epiglottis is no exception, and learns to distinguish between sea water for the lungs and gill slits, and fresh water for the stomach.

"So far, you have not been fed—which made the cold-water experiment you have just been through all the more effective."

Dodge had the insane desire to shout at the man, to hurl invective, to leap up there and tear him off his perch, to rend all the arrogant contempt of him. Then he remembered the shock-haired man. He had been allowed to make his protest, and had then been hauled off as a potential trouble-maker. A neat, if nasty, technique.

"Fish are equipped with what is known as a 'red body'. This extracts oxygen from the blood stream and passes it into the buoyancy bladder, thus enabling the fish to rise. The 'oval' removes the oxygen, and the fish sinks. Those organs of your body have been restored to you. Grafting is a fine art." The fellow was actually drooling over it all, over the macabre things that had been done to these men's bodies. Dodge felt the dull rage of anger burn through him.

"Your lungs are filled with oxygen when you wish to rise—and the normal oxygen-poisoning that takes place when oxygen is under nine-atmospheres pressure does not affect you, as those particular lung sections are not then being used for breathing purposes. I assure you, you will all feel perfectly at home undersea, and will work well. Any attempt at revolt will be met with instant suppression."

Dodge wondered vaguely whether he'd say that if you tried to escape you'd be shot, and if you tried again they'd flog you to death, and any subsequent attempt would meet an even worse fate. He couldn't even raise a smile.

The man lording it over them from his dais was wearing a full breathing set coupled in with his foam rubber dress. So he was all right. He wasn't condemned to breathe water for the rest of his natural life. Dodge's slow burning anger branded his mind; the injustice of it all ousted for a mad moment the phlegmatic acceptance he had schooled into himself during those bad hours in the cell. The slave-driver was speaking again, his amplified voice loud in the rocky chamber. A small piece of coral fell from the roof and drifted idly down. Automatically, men moved out of

73

the way. It might have been fire coral, and, with the normal death cycle of coral when the sun's light is dimmed in the depths being severely interfered with by men's artificial lighting—well, no one was taking chances.

"There is much work for you here. At first you will be employed in sheltered waters on the edge of the scarp. Later, you will go farther afield." A mocking note edged the condescending voice. "One other thing, before you go about your work. We have your welfare at heart. Good workers will be rewarded. Trouble-makers will be punished. Always remember, whenever you are mad enough to dream of revolt or flight, that both are impossible. Never forget that if you work well, you may be given the chance of further surgery which will let you breathe air. That should be your goal, towards which you strive." He held up a hand, beckoned.

Guards poured in, shepherded the slaves out and into a long mess hall with tables arranged neatly. No one needed to be told to eat. The food was vitamin rich, fatty, lots of sugar, all of it in forms which could be chewed without loss in the salty water. Developing the trick of swallowing without getting a stomachful of salt water took time and patience; at the end of the repast everyone was eating as fast as they could. They knew that food represented life.

Flippers were issued and as he adjusted his, Dodge acknowledged with a shock that penetrated his sombre, hating mood; that with the flippers on his feet he felt at home, as though some part of him had been made up —as though he had been missing a vital organ. He crushed the stupid desire to look at his hands in case his fingers were growing webbed.

He decided, irritably, that if anyone started quoting poetry about sea changes he'd invite him to change places. Although—anyone he met socially down here was likely to be in the same position as himself. He kicked off and flew moodily across to the assembly point. Someone's flipper caught him a blow on the arm and he turned, snarling—a facial grimace that, underwater, with the weak vocal cords of a human being, meant nothing. The culprit backed off, shook his hands together in apology, and darted off. Dodge flew on.

At the next issuing-point each man had a bell fixed

74

around his neck. The thing tinkled inanely away under his chin. But it wasn't in the least funny—sound would betray underwater far more than on the stillest night above ground. And that's what the bell was for. Dodge knew some of the many signs and gestures that had evolved in the silent world of undersea for communication; this particular bell did not fit into that particular category at all.

Guards and overseers bullied the men about, pushing them into lines, sorting them into teams. Dodge was thrust peremptorily into a group of ten others and under their foreman's impatient goading, ordered through into an upward sloping tunnel. Ceiling lights at intervals threw mercury gleams into the clear water and the heart-throb beat and thump of engines vibrated all around. He flew upwards, the infernal bell, a mocking tintinabulation under his chin, reminding him of captivity.

CHAPTER NINE

Like the opening of that manhole through which in dream he had fallen seen from the sewer, a round opening grew in size above him, first a sixpence, then a shilling and finally a half-crown. In the confines of the close-pressing tunnel the overseer halted the party and reached for a telephone set in a coral niche. Small fishes darted away in all directions. Two little fellows, no more than half an inch long, flew cheekily out of the mouthpiece.

It wasn't any telephone that could operate in air, Dodge saw. Really, it was a speaking tube, filled with water and with a diaphragm at each end. Sound vibrations traveled along the tube at nearly three thousand miles an hour, concentrated, perfectly private and inaudible to any listener whose ear was not clamped to the diaphragm. After a few moments conversation, the guard replaced the phone and the party resumed its upward climb.

A magnificent emerald green light filled the whole world when Dodge poked his head through the opening and wriggled out to stand on firm-packed sand. This was the cloaking atmospheric color brought into the deeps by Man. Before him stretched a fairyland of wonder, an enchanted garden, an underwater Eden on which the gates had been slammed long ago, leaving the serpent and its brood in undisputed possession. For a space the bottom was level, extending to the lip of the continental shelf and the great deeps beyond, and the entire area visible represented at once a scene of grandeur and impressive achievement, and a brooding sense of impending catastrophe, that nothing short of fresh air and sunshine could dispel.

Gigantic madreporic formations rose like a parody of a sunken city: crenelets, towers, battlements, pylons and arches sprawling in confusion, creating a labyrinth of life. Tiny coral fish, iridescent, flashed everywhere like jewels. Floating serenely in scarcely appreciable currents, tufts and blossoms of Alcyonaria, like candy-floss, moved like clouds. Above, the surface was quite out of sight, the blueness of the distant water seeming to extend to infinity. At the edge of vision vague shapes hovered. Directly above Dodge's head a blaze of yellow illumination came from a lamp suspended on tripod legs, and at regular intervals other lamps shed light onto the underwater world. The light, seen from a distance beyond thirty feet, assuming that deeply gorgeous emerald green so characteristic of artificial lighting in the undersea. And over everything, beyond the reach of the lamps, was draped the blue filter of the water, softening outlines, filling crevices with mysterious shadows, robbing everything not directly in a shaft of radiance, of its color and texture.

Men's limbs took on a ghostly sheen, as though rubbed in grease-paint. Faces and bodies glowed a pale greenish-blue, colors grayed and standardized in an aquamarine of pristine purity—and the brilliant strokes of hard primary color that showed on man-made objects and on coral and fish whenever they moved into range of the lights forced a glaring contrast almost indecent in its ripping away of the blue veil of mystery cloaking the watery continent.

A bed of human brains of monstrous size leered in intricate convolutions under his feet.

Shakily, Dodge forced his overstrained nerves to relax. Those animal growth, so like outsize human brains, were merely brain corals; but the first onslaught had given him a jolt.

Seaweeds of brilliant color vying with the hues of their coral hosts trailed away in riotous profusion. They swayed with a rhythmic abandon, lazily, in time with unfelt currents. The whole effect was of watching a garden in a movie projector that had been slowed down to quarter speed. It was eerie, compelling, utterly foreign and yet intensely familiar; Dodge recognized, with a deep sense of humility, that the sea and its marvels meant something to him now—with all the pain and misery and humiliation that that knowledge brought—that he could never have believed when he'd stepped from the spaceship on Earth.

The overseer waved an arm and the little party moved off. Everywhere in this undersea kingdom men flew, gliding down from upper working parties, toiling round a coral formation with compressed-gas hoses and drills, filing down into one of the many openings honeycombing the bottom. Some sandy patches, clear of marine growth, contained wire-mesh pens in which strange fish swam round and round, tirelessly, hungrily, restlessly.

Dodge knew that the seas had been through the upheaval of man's rearrangements; fish of types never before seen in familiar seas had been brought in and bred into huge, food-potent schools. Distribution of fish now was a headache to any orderly-minded ichthyologist. Food fish, in particular, what the slaves called sardines, had been forced to live in conditions unfamiliar to them, and with the ready promptness of all living things had quickly adapted over the generations. Perhaps the most outstanding change in fishy life had been the emphasis on depth. Now, coralled in their mile-wide pens, fish lived at depths in which, before the hand of man had been felt beneath the waves, they would have rebelled; retreated at once to their more familiar sunny waters of the surface. But all this aquiculture, this intensifying of nature's gifts along channels best suited to man, took place only above the continental plateaux. Out in the great waters the immense shoals of fish still enjoyed their age-old freedom of the seas.

Dodge, among his group of slaves, flew on over the undulating bottom, gliding now into a brilliantly lit area, sweeping on into the blue-shadow-land between lamps, and then veering to climb a coral wall and dive down to resume progress in this intoxicating extra dimension. Everywhere slave bells tinkled. A water-breathing man flew past slowly, his white smock emblazoned with a large cross, which, as he crossed an illuminated area, Dodge saw was red in color. The doctor was being towed by a large black-fin shark and the shark looked extraordinarily sorry for itself. The blackfins are not dangerous; it looked as though this specimen had run headon into something that was.

The doctor and his charge veered slightly to allow a swordfish to pass them. The swordfish had an ultra-sonic set attached to its back, just behind the head, and a set of harness fastened to its body. Two men with harpoons flattened themselves in the harness against the swordfish's side, and their steed bore them onwards with powerful strokes of its tail. As they vanished into the blue veil another team similarly equipped followed them.

Then came six younger tiger sharks, each a good twenty feet long, their tiger stripes showing up clearly as they swam through illuminated water. There were steel muzzles around their mouths, their wicked yellow eyes gleamed with a phosphorescent fire, chilling, and the man holding their six leads had a slender stick with which to prod them along.

Dodge began to thing that something was up.

A voice bellowed through the water.

"You there! Where do you think you're going?"

The overseer hauled up, his hand upflung to arrest the progress of his group. Dodge hung, motionless. Down towards them flew a burly, black-haired man wearing an armored vest of dural scales. Feet over head he came down like a furious thunderbolt. He held a compressed-gas repeater harpoon as though he knew what it had been designed to do.

"Reporting to Herring Pen Sixteen," the foreman said. He was puzzled.

"Haven't you heard, then?" The armored man sounded exasperated. He stopped just above the group of slaves, staring down on them. "The way they run things down there it's no wonder killers go off on the rampage."

"Rogues?" The foreman glanced uncertainly at his group. His hands gripped his harpoon nervously.

"Rogues, killers, we don't know yet what it is. Cut up a shark recce group, lost a couple of men, too." He motioned with the harpoon. "Sealed area ahead. You'd better go back and report to your boss. Pen Sixteen is too near the trouble area to have slaveys flying about in the way."

Shadows flitted across them and Dodge quite clearly

heard the thump of propellers. A small, two man sub, leaving a twisting tube of disturbed water behind it, sped past; men and fish clinging to it at every vantage point cadging a free lift. Six large fish that he did not recognize swam purposefully in rhythm together, towing a piece of underwater ordnance that looked like a giant hypodermic syringe equipped with balancing fins and rudder. Armored men streamlined themselves along the limber and gun. Outriders, mounted on swordfish, flanked the battery. All in all, Dodge realized with an uncomfortable rising excitement, this was a full-scale operation. Horse, foot and guns were going in.

The weirdness of it all, the bizarre conception of men riding fish, using killer sharks as hunting dogs, harnessing fish to haul cannon, all the bewildering possibilities open to underwater man, was lost on Dodge. He had a confused feeling that what was going on around him was unusual; but the human mind sets its own limitations on the amount of fresh experience a man can take. And after he had woken up to find himself breathing water, the circuits were full; no other panic messages could get through, nor would they for some time to come.

The foreman turned his ten men around and they all flew back to the same tunnel from which they had emerged. Dodge felt quite normal. There was no strain in flying underwater in his present condition, the surgical operation, whose details he didn't care to consider, had been thorough in its scope and he rose and fell effortlessly at the command of his new organs. He felt that the business about the cold, on the little amphitheater on the side of the continental plateau below, had a phoney ring. That guy, with his foam-rubber dress and his involved double-talk, had gone to a lot of trouble to sell the idea that the water was so cold it would invariably kill the slaves. Hell —he was flying in the same water now, wasn't he? Admittedly, it was shallower here; he was not flying over the profound deeps of the ocean bottom proper. But, still . . . He wished fervently that Harp was around to discuss things. They'd resolve the communication problem, all right. Just a bit of time and experiment, and man can solve almost anything, in the same way that he can adjust, and

80

come to accept as thoroughly normal, new experiences that would have driven him, unprepared, insane.

Adaptation demands time, it is no rapid, easy change. The inner spark that burns in every man, however lethargically he tends the flame which gutters flaringly in the winds of adversity; he finds new levels of his consciousness and personality and will light up; sometimes he draws fresh inspiration and sometimes he sees barrenness of spirit—and then the flame flickers and goes out. Adaptation and mutation are not the same; mutation may explode in a night but adaptation takes time.

He had the time. The days that followed, artificially divided by sleeping and waking and punctuated by eating, formed a pattern based on the first day. Wake up. Eat. Fly out to work. Tending the fish, looking after algae beds and cutting seaweeds, clearing coral encysted rocks, a hundred and one jobs forming the daily drudgery. Then back to the rocky cavern with its rickety bunks and their mattresses that poked at tired muscles as though filled with coral.

He wondered why his skin didn't go white and slough off, and discovered that their diet encouraged an oil skim over their own skin through the sweat pores. The excess of salt in their bodies from saltwater was not really an excess at all, the sweat secretions flushed salt out as though they were toiling in a sun-parched desert. Those calmly methodical devil-doctors who had done this to him thought of everything. He was growing tougher and stronger than he had ever been in his life, certainly more robust than when he'd floated around in spaceships in free fall.

Some slaves had secreted slates and chalky writing implements that allowed them to luxuriate in the splendors of communication. Just to receive the impression of another person's mind, new thoughts, outside interests, fresh viewpoints, was a precious experience, an asset to be hoarded and prized and defended against the raids of the guards. News circulated. Dodge soon became *au fait* with what went on in this Bishop Wilkins Corporation; but one significant fact did not escape his observation. No one knew the name of this company. Reason for that—he tried to hammer out in his own mind with a trembling approach to a logic that he thought had died forever—must be because there was a chance that the slaves could escape. The bosses did not want escaped slaves knowing who had taken and fettered them. And fettered was not dramatic! My God—what man with all the chains and balls in the stinking jails of the world was ever fettered as Dodge was chained now? But, escape—his mind ran on this secretive anonymity of the corporation. So there was a chance to get away! If only Harp were here . . .

Information on the Rogue that had caused his group to return on the first day was scanty. Whispers—in the form of hastily scribbled phrases—seeped around that a huge killer shark, all of forty-five feet long, was prowling the outer nets and corrals. Other rumors, correcting this to killer whale and then dismissing him, said that a cachalot whale had gone mad and was tearing through the pens and plankton factories leaving destruction in his wake. The lack of news with even a tang of authenticity was not only frustrating to Dodge—it was frightening. The world was spinning along to its destiny, and he was fumbling about mindlessly beneath the sea.

The rumor, small yet persistent, in which Dodge was interested, wishing to believe it, said that the trouble was the work of escaped prisoners living in a sunken wreck. Discounting all the romantic rubbish about sunken wrecks, the idea that someone—if merely men like himself who could breathe only water—were consciously seeking to communicate with the slaves, possibly to help them to escape, filled him with an indescribable glee. His hatred for the men who had done this unspeakable thing to him was so deep, so much a part of him, that he was no longer conscious of it. It manifested itself in his psychology, in the way he thought, in his glee that someone was out to damage the farms owned by the bosses. He rubbed his fins in anticipation.

He was put one day with a smaller party than usual, just the overseer and two other men who were unknown to Dodge. Their job was to clean out a large tank that had, at some time in the past, fallen, or been tipped over, and was now a living mass of marine growth. The task would not be pleasant, and the menfish had been issued with metal-reinforced rubber gloves and short-handled rakes. He saw the overseer tucking a first-aid kit into his pouch. Dodge knew all about sea urchins, fire coral and *pteoris volitans*—the firefish which looks like waving branches of coral until the rows of stingers go into action. Their poison causes such intense pain, Dodge had been warned at lectures, that a man could swim through boiling water without having his attention distracted.

All that merely pointed up what he had felt to be true as soon as he began to find his fins in this watery graveyard. Now that he was a manfish, sharing in the comings and goings of others like himself, his masters were taking greater care of him than ever they had done when he was merely slave labor equipped with an aqualung. He represented invested capital to them now. The surgical operation must be of titanic complexity and skill, capable of being performed only by a master of surgery equipped with the latest techniques.

Flying with sure practiced strokes of his flippers, his hands relaxed at his sides, Dodge considered the slave-state mentality and took comfort from the eventual downfall of every slave-based empire of the past. He had been aware within himself, these past days, of a growing acceptance of his future. He would not always be a slave. Certainly, he could never become a foreman, a lackey of the dryneck bosses. But there must be some niche he could fill—perhaps the Space Force could find employment for him on Venus—the delightful calculations of designing a spaceship to be pressurized with water flowed through his mind. He became absorbed. He was finding something of his old self; the spaceman who had roared out to Jupiter and ventured onto the sunside of Mercury. Commander Jeremy Dodge, Space Force, no longer existed; only Jerry Dodge, manfish, trying to work out some rational pattern for a future life of some use to himself and to humanity.

The encrusted tank loomed up out of the blue veil. Dodge did not know at what depth beneath the surface he and his mates were working; but sunlight reached the bottom here, filtered of all yellows and reds and violets. Just the all-pervading blue-green that cut down vision on days of good-seeing to sixty or seventy feet and on bad days, when the plankton stream had been diverted, for instance, to zero. He knew little enough about the technicalities of under ocean; but he felt convinced that the shelf where they worked must rise from the main continental plateau by a considerable distance. Maybe he was laboring in a favorable spot. Maybe he was lucky. He banged the rake on the tank meditatively. It rang like some drowned tocsin of the deep.

Wedges of fish criss-crossed, fleeting in all directions, their fins blurs of speed. These brilliant, picturesque, startlingly marked, inedible fish still flourished, undomesticated by man.

The overseer motioned with his harpoon and the three slaves began slowly to chip away at the encrustations. A single little fish, about six inches long, floated out of the top of the rectangular tank, turning its body slowly from side to side. The foreman's lamp threw a yellow globe of radiance, the beam of which was invisible, leaving only the rays' impact to show where it was directed. In that light the little fish gleamed like a priceless jewel.

Dodge stopped chipping to stare. The fish's bright blue body was banded by golden stripes, and its fins were a glittering, glorious gold. Dodge was spellbound. The fish showed no fear of him. It stood in the water, looking almost gravely at him. Dodge flicked his flippers and rose, glided towards the little fish. Momentarily, it stood its ground; then it backed off and Dodge was looking down into the tank.

He couldn't shout. He waved his arms, beckoning, and the others flew up to join him at once. In the tank lay a large shark.

Even as the menfish above looked down, the shark's widely grinning mouth opened. Critically, Dodge thought that the movement lacked the precise snap he had come to expect. Then he saw with shock the bunch of small fish clustered around the shark swim deliberately into the gaping mouth. He felt bewilderment at this mass voluntary suicide, this self-immolation. The fishes disappeared, the wide cruel blue and gold fish had gone in with the others. His bewilderment increased.

The overseer said: "Mother shark. Those are her nippers. Real mother love, these sharks have. Never believe it, you wouldn't, until you see it happen." He shifted position and dropped lower, harpoon at the ready. "Thought so. She's a goner. We'd better get those sharklets out and take 'em back to the nursery where they can be looked after."

The job was pathetically easy. The mother shark's strength had all gone, torn away by the hunger gnawing continually at all sharks, spurred by their huge, oversized livers. The little episode affected Dodge profoundly. Carrion eaters and scavengers of the seas, Dodge had always had a revulsion towards sharks; now he felt sympathy for their sad, ever-hungry fate as the young sharks were taken out and the dead mother left to moulder in the tank, her flesh and bones to be eaten away by the parasites of the seas. After all, sharks are an ancient, stupid life form; keeping up with the progress of other fishes around them is a tough task; they were more at home in the warm seas of a primeval world.

The four menfish flew back, herding the panicky little sharks, lines quickly lashed round their tails. Dodge became aware of a dark shadow flicking about just about his area of vision. He lifted his head. Riding his pressure wave was the blue and gold fish.

"Oh, no!" Dodge said to himself. "I'm caught! I've inherited a pilot fish!"

It wasn't a remora, a sucker fish, so there was no chance that it would stick itself to him and refuse to let go until its head came off. He tried to shoo it away; but the little devil stuck to him persistently, riding around him, bobbing along on his pressure wave, sliding down between his legs and coming up, as cheekily as you like, on the other side. Eventually, Dodge gave up and philosophically paddled back.

Anyway, he was far too immersed in thought about the main item he had seen in the tank to be for long distracted. That dying mother shark, pathetic, sad, had given him food for thought. He had seen, studding the flat head, a pattern of tiny upright sticks. What they were he did not know. Touching them had told him they were metal; metal needles. The shark's head was a mass of such needles. Lying on the floor of the tank had been a plastic, streamlined cover, and Dodge would bet everything he hoped for that that plastic cover had fallen off the bed of needles—it might have even caused the shark's death. He shook his head. There was something here that must have a direct bearing on the control of fish. He had an idea what the system was, now, and he schemed how he could turn the information to his own benefit. He refused to see the ludicrous side of the picture, a man cut off by dumbness from his fellows, discovering a small facet of the methodical control of fish and determining to do something about it. For the sake of his own restless energy he had to have a focus for his scheming and dreaming.

All the way back the brilliant little pilot fish frisked about him.

The water was growing imperceptibly darker. It became noticeable only when a distance did not match up to a mental estimate of it. Far above them the sun's rays were slanting ever more steeply on the face of the deep; soon the sun would sink beneath the horizon, but long before then utter darkness would enfold the depths. By that time all menfish, who were not on outside duty, would be shut up in their rocky cells, eating their ample meal and making wearily for their beds. Dodge went through the whole procedure mechanically, and his little pilot fish went as faithfully through the same procedure. Dodge tossed it a morsel of food and the little beggar snapped it up and grinned for more.

That settled the issue. He had acquired a pilot fish for life. It was his own personal satellite. He decided to call it Sally.

Dodge and Sally flew off to his cell, angling down through the water-filled tube beneath the ground. A file of menfish was ascending, and the slaves pressed to one side to allow the armored and armed menfish to brush roughly past them. The night patrol, equipped with heated suits and lamps and asdic, these men carried out a prowl guard of the rim all the hours of the night. Dodge was paying them little attention, automatically keeping his legs clear of the too-freely brandished harpoons.

With a sense of shock as deep as any he had experienced since his awakening as a manfish, he saw Harp in the midst of the patrol.

He moved forward involuntarily, his face lighting up.

Harp was clad in a scaled, heated suit, with the twin

headlamps on his forehead giving him a gargoyle look of power. He had a seven-shot compressed-gas harpoon, one of the magnum models, and the way he handled it told Dodge that Harp had found some surcease from agony.

The frustration of dumbness maddened Dodge. He grimaced. He grinned. He waved his arms.

Harp looked at him. Harp said: "Out of the way, slavey. Or I'll tickle you with this spear." He thrust the harpoon forward. Blankly, Dodge fell to one side.

He flapped his arms frantically, opening his mouth, forming words. This couldn't be!

Harp frowned. "Get out of the way, slavey!"

Dodge felt the prick of the harpoon. He pressed against the rock wall, watching Harp fly on, the muscles rippling across his thighs, his gill slits opening and closing like narrow mouths laughing at him. Even in that moment of utter horror, the sight of the gill slits across back and under arms brought the fleeting thought of the master surgery needed to bypass the interlacing intercostal muscles. It tantalized Dodge with his own helplessness.

Dodge floated there a long while, looking blindly down the tunnel after Harp. And when he turned to fly back to his bunk, his face was as hard as the rock about him.

CHAPTER TEN

Pulling off his facemask, Captain Pinhorn, Space Force, looked disgustedly at Pierre Ferenc, U.O.P. Water gurgled away through the gratings beneath their feet and Pinhorn had to catch himself, consciously take stance upon his legs, as the buoyant support flowed away. Gleaming blue and orange from reflected light, the air-pressure dials on the chamber's metal walls showed that the men were breathing at twenty-one atmospheres. It was enough to make a regular spaceman's hair curl; but Pinhorn recognized the basic sense underlying all the simplicities and short-cuts he'd come up against since he'd been undersea. When you live six hundred feet beneath the sea there is little point in going through decompression stages every time you climb out of the water. Pinhorn gave a little shiver and wiped his face off with a paper towel from the dispenser. Ferenc's classic features received a perfunctory wipe of his hands.

"It's all very well for you chaps who live and work down here," Pinhorn said protestingly. "I've got a job to do. I came here . . ."

"—especially from the Moon on important Space Force assignment," Ferenc finished for him. He punched the other's bicep. "I know, Pin, but what can I do? You've seen the guv'nor. Now we wait until this Grosvenor guy arrives."

"Well, he's taking long enough," grumbled Pinhorn.

Both men walked through to the mess; in the warmed

and sterilized air they neither needed or wanted any more clothing than their swimming trunks. Pinhorn had had a little trouble adjusting to the weird sound distortions consequent on speaking in a helium-oxygen atmosphere—the Space Force with no high-pressure problems used plain old air—but with the facility of a technical man he had painstakingly and thoughtfully overcome the difficulty, and could now converse like a grown adult and not a child yelling down the echoing-corridor of a mouldering castle. He hated to have to admit it; but these underwater boys were on the ball.

Simon Hardy bustled in, jerking his amputated left arm, smiling, talking energetically, trailed by Minister of Aquiculture George Werner.

"So you see, George," Hardy said non-stop with a quick nod of his head to Ferenc and Pinhorn. "If we round up the northern whale herds early in the season it means we have a better chance of saving more calves from the scavengers—killer whales, sharks—you know what goes on up there just as well as I do. We're losing far too many head of whale for my liking."

"You were only saying the other day, Simon, that you didn't have the personnel . . ."

"Fiddlesticks! Of course I haven't the personnel! It's precisely because of that I want to round up the northern herds early. I'll use all the Rangers on it, then they can all move south for . . ."

"For your own damn pet schemes, eh, Simon?" said Henderson, walking in with a smile, and a camera slung round his neck. A heavy diving knife of beryllium-bronze, along with photographic equipment, was strapped to his belt over the scrappy shorts. His body shone with water; old he might be, like Hardy and Werner, but, like them, he was in the pink of condition. Claiming the seas for humanity had entailed going into it with fair frequency, and not just sitting importantly behind a leather-covered desk and initialling reports. He flung a small harpoon gun onto a side table. "You want to use those men to ferret around in the Juliana Trench, right?"

"Too right," growled Hardy. He sat at the table and picked up his Nelsonian knife-fork. "We've got to lick whatever it is lurking down there."

Pinhorn's ears pricked up and his face assumed the carefully blank stare of a man listening avidly, whilst concealing that fact lest the talkers should realize his presence and keep silent. Anything he could learn about Under Ocean would be of great interest to Toxter of the Space Board. Pinhorn knew well enough of the continual bitter battle for appropriations that went on in UN, and was aware that the last fiscal enquiry had resolved nothing.

Werner was speaking. Pinhorn had him sized-up by this time and knew that under the fat, roly-poly body and face and limp handshake was a quicksilver mind, alert and open to new ideas—very much a man of the background whose words would carry more weight than all the bellowings of, say, a Toxter. "I agree that it would be desirable to carry out the round-up early. But this other business . . ." he shook his head doubtfully.

Henderson began eating with relish. Waving a fork in the air and using it to stab each punctuation mark, he said: "Now look here, Simon. We've got to trash this out. We three here put aquiculture on the map. Oh. I'm not harping on the same old tune, I know others talked about it for years; but we three did it!" His voice became persuasive. "We have to stick together, put a combined front on our actions, show UN that we mean business." He glanced keenly at Pinhorn. "I'm sure that Captain Pinhorn will not take it the wrong way; but we all know that Space and Ocean are in conflict; under our blessed system that is inevitable. There just isn't enough money and material to go round."

Pinhorn inclined his head. Any remark would be superfluous.

Hardy broke in bluntly: "That means that we have to safeguard our own interests." His eyes narrowed on Pinhorn. "I don't want to sound vicious, you understand; but don't you think it would be a good idea if we refrained from discussing this with a Space Force officer present?"

Immediately, Pinhorn rose. Henderson put out a hand and pressed him back into his seat.

"Go on with your meal, captain. What we have to discuss here will soon be no secret from the world, let alone from Space Force Intelligence."

"You mean you're releasing the news?" demanded Hardy.

"Well," Henderson temporized. "It's this way, Simon. I'm not at all happy about the way in which Under Ocean has been running lately. You and I and George share a common ideal, the opening up of the seas of the world for the good of humanity. But others don't see things that way." He smiled a little bitterly and laid the fork down. "Perhaps we've gone on living too long. Perhaps geriatrics didn't do so wonderfully well as we'd thought; perhaps old fogeys like us should have died off and left the seas to the younger, smarter, more ruthless boys. We began the great ideal and almost before we'd realized that we'd swung it, it was snatched from us by people I'm ashamed to know live undersea. We gave the snowball its initial push and now its gone rushing off without us, smashing up people and lives and Heaven-knows what." His dark, nervous face showed mounting strain as his mind reviewed the prostitution of a dream.

"Not everybody . . ." began Werner.

"I mean some of these pettifogging little Bishop Wilkins Corps! We all know what goes on. Men press-ganged from seaside resorts, taken up at sea, even trapped in inland river towns. Turned into slaves. They've hung the charter of the UN up in the toilet. And the internecine warfare that goes on between the companies, raids and counter-raids, emphasis on profit and get-rich-quick and easy living, instead of getting the most out of their concessions. I'm sick of it all!"

"Aren't we all!" Hardy said hotly, banging down his knife-fork and ignoring the obvious distress in Werner's abruptly checked movement to reach across to Henderson. "But the system is running now. It's in full swing."

Henderson rubbed a hand across his face and smiled at Werner. Werner allowed a quick tilt of his mouth to betray satisfaction, and turned his attention to Hardy. Deliberately, he took a forkful of food. "And if we tried to change it in mid-stream," he said, his mouth full, "we'd have the biggest famine the world's ever seen on our hands."

"But we're going to change it," snapped Hardy.

"That's right, Simon." Henderson had regained what

91

normal self-control a man of his nervous temperament ever has. He picked up a fish bone and nibbled the meat that tasted like chicken. His tones were deceptively soft. "But how do you propose to do that?"

Pinhorn's attention darted between the diners like a dragon-fly over a clump of water flowers. He was stimulated, aroused—these men were alive, vital, almost as good as the spacemen he knew so well. A pity they— well, he supposed it had been a fortunate circumstance these men had taken up Under Ocean. At least, they'd got something done. Pinhorn's food lay before him, untasted.

"I'll tell you how," Hardy said violently. "Give me more men, more equipment, more subs. We'll move in on one of the biggest undersea farms and break the system there by a mass onslaught. That's about the only way. Then we'll prosecute in camera so as not to flush the rest of the game, and then move on to the next."

"How long will that take, Simon?"

Hardy lifted his attenuated left arm and stared at it as though it had just happened. "Hell of a while."

"Precisely." Henderson put the fish bone down delicately. "Right. Here's what we do. And we'll need Pinhorn's help. We do just as you said before, Simon, in connection with the Juliana Trench."

"The Juliana Trench! But you vetoed that idea before! After I said I wanted to broadcast it to the world you said the plan was utterly impracticable. Those were your very words; 'Utterly Impracticable.' Now what?"

"Just as you planned, Simon. But with one big difference. Since I've been down here in Trident I've been mooching around—you know, browsing here and there, talking to officers and men, finding out all kinds of little things that I couldn't pick up stuck out there on top of that damned UN skyscraper. Things that you'd told me truly enough, but I'd never integrated into a coherent whole in my own mind. And they all add up to just one thing."

Werner stopped eating and looked expectantly at Hardy. Pinhorn guessed that he knew what was coming and was awaiting the crusty old undersea fighter's reaction to the coming bombshell.

Around the table, neatly set with its silver and plastic, the tension screwed up; Ferenc lifted his head to stare at his chief and then, slowly, to turn and look at Henderson. Werner touched his lips with a napkin and then tossed it crumpled onto the cloth. Pinhorn waited impatiently. Somewhere out of sight a messman dropped a plate and the clatter served as a gong, announcing the curtain.

Henderson said: "Have you ever thought just who are, or is, this thing or things in the Juliana Trench, Simon?"

Hardy let out a gust of air.

"Well, of course! Deep-sea currents, probably. But I still think that my idea of some antagonistic life-form down there has a strong basis of truth. There just might be. We saw pictures of vague forms, outlines, something, when sub Nine went down. You've seen the recordings."

"They said someone was knocking to be let in."

"Well, you know what can happen to men's minds under the strain of that sort of situation."

"That officer struck me as being a very brave man. I think he was right."

"You—what?"

"I think, and my added observations here lead me to suppose that I may not be far wrong, that a life form lives in the Juliana Trench." Henderson paused. Then he said slowly, with quiet, chilling emphasis: "A life form with intelligence."

A little babble of talk burst out round the table. Pinhorn felt a roaring in his ears. Ferenc was sitting, his face chalk-white, his hands gripped into fists. Werner's eyes were fastened like two remoras to Hardy's face.

Henderson sat back and pounded the table with his knife. He was smiling now, a genial, friendly smile; with all the coldness in it of the water under the North Pole.

"Gentlemen. That is only half the story."

Silence.

Henderson looked squarely at Pinhorn,

"Captain Pinhorn, Space Force. When you report the subject of this little conversation to your superiors, or to Mr. Toxter, would you kindly add that Henderson, of Ocean, also thinks that the intelligent life form living in Earth's own ocean did not originate on this planet?"

Mr. Grosvenor, anyone could see at a glance, was a very worried man. Very worried indeed. He sat obesely in the speeding flying-carpet watching the ground unreel beneath the pulsing jets, and beat his fingers on his thighs in unconscious rhythm with them. His personal pilot, up front, did not look round, although Grosvenor had the irritable feeling that the fellow knew just what was going on in the rear of the craft. The ducted fans whirled merrily beneath his feet, spewing air downwards and lifting the ship so that her jets could hurl her through the air at better than four hundred miles an hour—a nicely sedate speed for the mood Grosvenor was in.

They were heading directly into the sunset—and umber and ochre burnt all along the horizon.

Air? Grosvenor hated the stuff. His skin felt itchy, his eyes burned and his throat ached. His skin was covered with sweat, and he had torn off his collar and tie and flung them beside him on the seat. His nervousness smelt.

What did that shark-bait Hardy want, anyway? Who said he had the right to demand that Grosvenor should come to him? Ever since Arthur Dodge had died there had been nothing but toil and trouble. Here he was, talented, highly respected, eminently successful; worked carefully and methodically—if perhaps, he acknowledged complacently, a trifle ruthlessly—to rise from a computer-tending clerk to manager of a large and rich Wilkins Corporation with everything yet to be, the future a rosy haze of golden opportunities—well, there would have been fine pickings there. But things had not gone at all as he had planned. And when his secretary, Elise Tarrant, began getting ideas of her own, that had been the final humiliation. Grosvenor was not prepared to truckle to any pipsqueak little miss just out of pigtails. Mind you, she was quite a dish—Grosvenor moved his fat shoulders against the backrest and dwelt for a moment on the contours of Miss Tarrant—quite a dish.

He rubbed the nose that had been sculpted by a whisky bottle—used internally—and tried to think of more pleasant things than either Simon Hardy or Miss Elise Tarrant. Inevitably, his seething thoughts veered round to that stupid Space Force Commander Dodge. Trust an old rip like Arthur Dodge to have a dimwit for a nephew.

The thought of his unanswered letters to Jeremy Dodge was a sore point with Grosvenor. It smacked too much of open contempt, and if there was one thing that Grosvenor's pride, the feeling within him that he had had so carefully to nurture—of being just as good as the next fellow in his climb to success—could not stand, that hackle-raising attitude was contempt. If the fellow had even offered to call in the police—or the U.O.P.— Grosvenor would have understood and got a line on the man's makeup. But dumb, insolent silence, ever since he'd landed on the Moon—well, Grosvenor had known what to do then, by George, he had!

The flying carpet swooped down towards the coast.

Soon his private sub would be taking him out to U.O.P. Base Trident, and to Admiral Hardy with his white helmet of hair and hard teakwood face and stupidly flapping left arm. The shark who had done that had been too damned slow for Grosvenor's liking. And Mr. Grosvenor's face muscles tautened and his fingers beat a distressing tattoo on the seat.

If only he knew where Elise Tarrant and young Dodge were now! If only he knew where the hell they'd got to!

CHAPTER ELEVEN

One thing Sally wouldn't do was go near the bell hung round Dodge's neck.

Apart from that, she was the nearest—and dearest—thing in Dodge's life. He recalled that they used plain ordinary bicycle bells up near the surface to call the fish come feeding time; down here there were all manner of electronic devices. Dodge had quickly found the power sources of the undersea world. There was one hydrogen-power station, sited in an immense sunken mountain, and taking up nearly all of it with shielding necessary to deal with the colossal temperatures raised. Most everyday power was drawn from underwater river turbines.

He'd been incredulous at first; but he soon found there were mightier rivers beneath the sea than all the Amazons and Congos and Niles of the upper world.

As an interesting example of the methods of the Bishop Wilkins farming fraternity—they were told at lectures that any slave who allowed himself to be caught in an upcurrent and washed too near the surface would be dealt with in the poisons tank. The slaves wouldn't get away, of course; the guardian fish with their electronic and asdic devices would see to that, quite apart from the miles of wire fencing hemming them in. But the poisons tank —Dodge had seen this horrific contraption when he'd been ordered to take a message capsule to a guard stationed there. The tank was filled with a varied and nauseating collection of all the poisonous fauna of the seas, ranging from fire coral and jelly-fish up to giant sting rays. Most of the poison fish weren't in themselves horrible; the effects they unwittingly caused, under the direct goading of men-fish in authority, gave rise to feelings of revulsion and terror.

Luckily for Dodge's nerves and stomach—for this poisons tank was far, far worse than the one he'd seen when he'd been an aqualunger—no poor devil of a run-away slave had been tossed in whilst he was there.

He had an irrational and soul-destroying fear of the stonefish, the killem-on-the-spot kid of the coral reefs. He never saw one, which might, had he troubled to puzzle it out, have shown him he wasn't in Australian waters. Like all underwater menfish, he disliked touching exposed coral walls unless he knew exactly what he was doing. Even so, at the end of the shift the menfish usually formed a cursing, complaining queue at the first aid room, having cuts and abrasions disinfected and plastic skin sprayed on. In salt water you didn't notice the sting of a cut when it happened; Dodge had often been surprised to find gashes and scratches on arms and legs when he got back to his cell.

One of the biggest queries of all was just exactly where on the globe was he? That query, posed nakedly like that, might have aroused ribald mirth among the guards. Not that they knew where they were, either; but their answer, with a curse and a blow, would have been: "You're in the sea, slavey. In the sea!"

It was useless trying to judge where they were by the fish.

Man had carried out as drastic a domestic upheaval in the seas as he had on land; greater, if anything, when the ease of herding animals in a medium that was interrupted neither by mountain ranges nor ocean barriers was fully appreciated. Whenever Dodge was out herding fish, or doing any of the man tasks directly connected with fish, as opposed to the work around the sea floor among the coral and weeds and algae, he tried to draw comfort from the thought that he was actively engaged in putting food into the larder of the world. It was easier to imagine that with fish; even though algae and weeds provided almost as much actual consumable food, apart from their commercial uses. But it was a thankless task. He felt no kinship whatsoever with the sheepherders, the cattle ranchers, the pig breeders of the upper, sunlit world. The mystery and wonder of the blue depths, its sudden changes of mood and color, its incessant movement and vitality of life; all were so different from any above water experience, that they spoke eloquently that here man was continually alone. A cowpoke looks across the rolling backs of the mighty herds of the prairies, and among the dust and sweat he can encompass his charges and his responsibility. Under the sea, a manfish flies along the flanks of his wavering silver-mirroring shoals, barred from vision by the blue eye-absorbing curtain, and can see only a fraction of his charges.

And yet, there was a remote kinship of a sort, but one which Dodge did not appreciate, one for which he was not yet prepared, one which, had he recognized it, he would have instantly rejected.

The strongest and most persistent information Dodge received, scrawled on slates late at night in the cell blocks, was that they were somewhere in the South Atlantic. He had nothing by which to judge the accuracy of this, his knowledge of the undersea world in a comparative sense was nil; and to counter-balance the South Atlantic theory were other guesses—South Pacific, Timor, Indian Ocean, even a wild and almost frivolous suggestion of the Red Sea.

Privately, Dodge leaned towards the Caribbean.

He'd been worried recently by a peculiar singing noise in his ears and had been to see the medical officer who had questioned him sharply, suspecting a malingerer, and then, after a perfunctory inspection, had packed him off to work with a stern admonishment that further sick-parades were functions he would do well to steer clear of —for reasons of health. The oddly disturbing drone in his ears persisted. He wondered, not without a pang of fear, if his eardrums were succumbing to the underwater life of continual changes of pressure. That his internal pressure balanced the outside water he knew; that the human cell, being nearly all water, was virtually incompressible he also knew; that sea water was so like blood that in some special circumstances it could act like blood he knew, too; but none of that served to cheer him up. His ears still ached.

He knew that he imagined more changes of pressure than there actually were; probably during an average day's work he might rise or fall a hundred feet which, at their depth beneath the surface, was thoroughly incapable of comparison with similar changes in depth at the surface waters. But he did have pressure changes upon him, both from within and without.

Among the other menfish with whom he worked and shared his days there was none he could really find it in his heart to be friendly with; the sad experience with Harp he thought had cured him of sentimental attachments of that sort. He could not bear to think of Elise; he consoled himself in silent communion with Sally, his glittering pilot fish, and found nothing strange or pathetic in the situation. At least, fish don't have tongues, and Elise had been mighty free with hers.

The classic remedy for painful ears, swallowing to open the Eustachian tubes, was useless when you breathed water—for one thing you didn't need to keep opening them when you lived permanently undersea. He'd been told that the operation had taken care of the ears; providing oxygen from the lung sections that were the swim bladder; but he was worried. At last, he communicated his ear trouble to a fellow slave in his group. He scrawled quickly: "Ears hurt."

In shaky, almost illegible writing—they were crouched down behind a coral bommie during a blasting operation and the overseer was far too busy playing with his little red and black wires and boxes—"Hurt? Or noises?"

Disturbed and strangely excited, Dodge scribbled: "Noises." Then he added: "Singing."

"I know. Me too. Lots of menfish."

"What is it?"

"Don't know."

And that was where he had to leave it, as the bommie shook and pieces of coral splattered and clumps of dead fish fluttered to the bottom with blood staining the water from their gills. It wasn't a pain. It did not inconvenience him at all, and, now that he thought about it, the doctor had not appeared in the least surprised. He must have many such complaints. The blasting they had just done had been felt by the menfish only mildly through the water—they were well outside the danger area. But, perhaps an accretion of explosions . . . ? It was just an occupational disease.

And then one day a miracle occurred.

Rather, two miracles; the second more wonderful than the first.

For some time Dodge had been aware that he was regarded with some favor by his foreman, and although the feelings aroused in him were a mixture of repugnance and hesitant hope, he did nothing to hinder his own advancement. But when he, and another score of menfish he did not know, were paraded under armed guards and flown to a warm water-filled niche on the inner face of the reverse scarp, facing the shore all those miles away, and were told what was expected of them—a wild elation surged through him. He was being offered the chance to carry a spear. He was told that he could volunteer —ironical word—to join the martial forces to combat the predators ravaging the outer rim.

Another boss talked to them, handling his words with semantic care, quite different in style from the first one who had told them their fate; but burdened by the same conscious knowledge of superiority. They were being given this chance because they had proved good, reliable workmen. Their food ration would go up. They would have better quarters. They would wear heated armored scale suits when on duty. They would become members of the elite—after a short probationary period, of course. This was the first step on the ladder of promotion that would lead to the operation that enable them to breathe air again.

The last, no one believed.

But the opportunity of better conditions, different work from the soul-destroying menial labor of the fish pens and the seaweed groves and algae beds, acted on them like a tonic. Knowing that he was a gullible, rather contemptible fool, Dodge accepted. He decided to become shark-fodder, as the spear-carriers were known with ironic truth among the menfish.

He was given a slap-up meal, issued with a suit of

armor and given a couple of hours' instruction with a ten-foot spear. The first moments with the weapon aroused a maelstrom of emotions within him. He was aware of the watchful guards, like sentinel sharks, scanning all the volunteers, their harpoons ready. Suddenly, Dodge was filled with the desire to go on living; it shook his whole body with a violent spasm; he would go along with these lordly overseers and bosses, play it their way, until the time came for the reckoning. Meanwhile, he practiced with the spear at towed targets, learning the knack of leverage and control, of thrust, learning to hurl the lance with the minimum of effort and maximum of control. He became an expert pikemanfish. And every savage thrust with the weapon he stored up in the barrel of hatred that curdled in his breast.

Very soon after that they were flown out to the outer reef and on the way the second and greater miracle came to pass.

Dodge had, like the other slaves, found difficulty in accustoming himself to the feel of clothes on his body. The scale armor, tough and flexible, yet chafed him over his brief trunks. Fumbling with a buckle, he caught his spear in a clump of widely branching coral and lagged behind the others to free it. Their tow, a large and docile nurse-shark—swam lazily on into the blueness. Edible fish were never used as beasts of burden, or as carriage animals, except on rare occasions, and the menfish slapped sharks and swordfish around as though they were donkeys. Dodge gave a sharp jerk; but the spear remained entangled.

The little bell hanging from the chain around his neck, symbol of the slave, had been removed when he had joined the ranks of the soldiers, and he had been issued with a bicycle bell which was worn strapped to the right arm. A simple code of signals had been taught them. Now, Dodge rang to say he had been delayed. The sergeant in charge shouted back to follow as soon as possible. So they trusted him then!

Not that there was much trust about it. All around him was the busy life of the undersea world, menfish coming and going, finning along on various errands, orderly shoals of fish being driven from pen to pen, inquisitive sharks nosing everywhere, shouts of overseers, the flash and glint of fins in the lights, the grumbling crunch of sundering coral as fresh beds were cleared. Just the working activity carried on every day in the inner baileys of any Bishop Wilkins undersea farm drowned in the bell-haunted deep.

Away to his left a deep cleft opened in the sea bed. Above it the water was laced by the waves of subs and skates and undulating flippers. Below, deep within the cleft, he could see single lights like orange stars. They were using a compressed-gas hose down there and as the light bubbles rose in a gushing stream, each one merged with its neighbor until, rising swiftly, they separated, grew, distended into swollen balls. They looked like spinning galaxies of stars, fire engorged, swirling past him and surging upwards. His eyes, following them, were jerked back below, as the lurid light below seemed to be smoking, to be sending off jets of fire. The spectacle was quite common, he had seen it a hundred times; yet now, struggling to free his spear, he saw it all again with the fresh eyes of youth.

By the time he had the spear free and started finning after the others, he had decided to take his time. There had never before been an opportunity to wander at will among the fairyland of grottoes and trailing seaweeds and clouds of tiny brilliant fish. Always, there had been the prod of authority, emphasized by the sharp spear point. Now—he carried a spear. He turned on his side and slanted down a long coral wall, aware of the danger he was courting and scarcely bothered what the sergeants would say—the wonder of freedom had gone to his head; he felt intoxicated by it.

He knew nothing of the scientific terminology of the fish and other animals of the sea; the slaves had their own vocabulary of names, most obscene, some funny, some the only obvious ones—as one ludicrous little fish that had a square body with eyes, mouth and tail apparently stuck on at random, which could only be called a box fish. In direct contrast there was the hula-hula fish, a graceful form with waving transparent fins.

When, in the yellow light from a pendant globe, Dodge saw the little burst of scarlet, he knew at once what it was. Looking like a firework display, the fire-fish extended its long poison spines, barely moving in the crevice of coral beneath Dodge's fins. In the general blueness among surrounding anemones, lichens, barnacles, its camouflage was perfect. Without that artificial light, Dodge could not be sure he would have perceived it. Before, when any dangerous creature had been met undersea, he had had to call for help. Now—he gave a savage thrust with the spear, impaled the deadly fire-fish and watched stoney-eyed as it died. A little blood tufted away in the water. Two sharks nosed up as Dodge scrubbed the dead body from the spear against a branch of coral.

He turned his back on them and flew off, along the sunken wall, entering regions he had never previously visited.

An odd feeling buzzed in the back of his brain. Understanding flashed so quickly that he jerked to a quivering halt. Sally, flung unprepared from his pressure wave, circled glittering, as though admonishing him.

However viciously atavistic had been the feeling when he'd killed the poison fish, it had released a valve in his mind that had been jammed. However unpleasant the truth, he had to face the fact that he felt wonderful now that he was no longer the lowest creature of the low. As a slave, there had been no one in a worse situation than he. Psychologically, there had been nothing on which to unload his own angers. Sally, he knew bemusedly, was a friend, dumb, barely intelligent, but so beautiful as to dispense with the need for anything else she yet gave him that priceless gift of companionship. However he looked at it, bad, cruel, wrong, completely primeval it might be; but killing the fire-fish had given him back an interest in life—in his own life.

His own psychological reactions were in some *outre* way similar to the cycle of life in the depths. The plants, living only in the upper sun-reached waters produced the first link by photosynthesis; and gradually, as the animals living on plants and each other grew larger, the food cycle was carried on, with the falling detritus on which the benthypelagic fish eked out their existence in turn being swept by upward currents back to the continental shelves.

Sally cavorted around him darting past his face and

body like an excited dragon-fly. Dodge chuckled. He felt now that life would open up, that there would be a way out of this whole mess; he waggled his spear and flew on along the wall, angling to reach the assembly point on the rim. Beyond that dividing line between the shelf and the deep sea, out in the blue, who knew what opportunities might not arise?

A warmly glowing radiance turned the atmosphere emerald green; as he flew nearer the light grew orange and angry, then turned yellow and he saw that it fell from a long row of round portholes in the nearly vertical lichen-covered rockwall. Interested, he flew closer. Sally backed off, flickering her golden fins. Screwing up his eyes he could see through the portholes rooms, corridors, a whole undersea city. It reminded him vividly of the Blue Deep Hotel, back there in the safety of shallow coastal waters.

Like the Blue Deep, this hotel, too, looked as though it were air filled. Dodge could not be sure. His excitement at the discovery grew. This must be all reserved area, places where the bosses lived, the men who were not menfish, the men who ordered and controlled and employed the miserable slaves like himself. Angrily, he struck with his spear at the plastic.

Reaction was prompt.

A woman wearing a pair of shorts and a brief jacket walked idly across, pressed her nose against the glass. She saw Dodge, hanging there in the water on his fins, and her excited signals brought other women crowding. They stared like fish in a tank. The truth shook him. He was the fish in the tank, he was the prisoned captive of the aquarium. These people could breathe air—they had millions of cubic miles of it to breathe above the surface of the world. He began to make faces at them and they laughed, delighted.

He inched along the row of portholes, peering in, chained there by a growing curiosity. As for the women —stupid giggling parasites. He would not allow himself to think. The women followed him until a wall barred them from the next porthole. Inside that room two men lay asleep. He passed on, flicking his fins quietly.

When he saw her at last he leaned his forehead against the transparent plastic and looked for a long while.

She was sitting in a bentwood chair, her head sunk in her hands, elbows on a wooden table. Lura, the little Siamese girl, was asleep on a bed. Their room was nothing but a cell and Dodge could see the bars, high up on the door.

Gently, he tapped his spear against the porthole.

There came no reaction from the girl at the table. Dodge struck again, impatiently, and drew his spear back sharply for another blow, and a shadow glided between him and the window. A large shark, attracted by Dodge's quivering movements, had sailed over to investigate. Its tiny brain, housed in a cartilaginous sheath, its stupidity and bumbling inquisitiveness infuriated Dodge at this crucial moment. He banged the shark over the head with the butt of his spear and the frightened beast, moon-mouth querulous, swirled away and vanished in the blue-ness. Dodge, breathing heavily, hammered on the porthole.

Elise lifted her head listlessly; no doubt she was accustomed to fish and men banging on her window; looked out —and saw Dodge.

The crystal magic of that moment contained a depth of feeling and meaning that Dodge could not encompass or understand. They looked at each other—the enchanted moment extending indefinitely, as though they mounted a silver stairway under a haunted sky, and through all the roaring in his brain there was only the pale face of Elise in all the world and nothing else at all—nothing else at all.

There were vivid yellow and violet anemones clustered round the window and trailing seaweeds vibrated gently across the pane. Tiny fish, no larger than postage stamps, fluttered like wind-tossed confetti and from beneath a coral overhang a blue crab with magnificent intaglio designs on his shell snapping his nippers merrily.

Elise said: "I thought—You're all right?" Her voice came, soft and musically muffled, through the window and the sea. Dodge nodded his head. He formed words with his mouth, laboriously, anxiously.

"You—all—right?"

"Yes." She passed a hand across her forehead. "Oh yes, we're all right here. Treated like lambs for the slaughter." She tried to smile. "So far, we've held out."

Dodge thought: *Thank God.*

He repeated it to himself over and over. He mouthed: "Escape?"

He had to form the word again and then Elise said: "No hope of that, Commander. No hope at all. Lura and I tried and didn't get as far as the airlocks. No one seems to know where we are—It's all my fault." Her face was ghastly.

Dodge shook his head. He rapped peremptorily on the window. "Not—your—fault. We'll—get—out."

How, was another matter, with the impenetrable barrier between them of air and water. Beyond Elise's shoulder he saw the door open and simultaneously the Siamese girl leap from the bed and fling herself at the handle, struggling to slam the door. Elise swung around, one hand to her throat. Dodge stared, horrified.

The door shuddered, then wrenched inwards. Lura dragged on the floor. A man shouldered in, a slender man with an unpleasant weasel face and yellow uneven teeth. His blubber lips lifted in a grimace as he saw Elise standing there, rigid, one hand half outstretched before her, the other at her throat. For some reason he could not explain, Dodge had flung one hand before his face, shielding it, so that he stared at this arrogant rodentlike man through slitted fingers.

Weasel-face saw Dodge, floating there outside the porthole. His face went mean. He rushed forward, shouting something obscene, clawing for Elise. Dodge had a quite distinct sensation of boiling-oil engulfing his guts. He was quite helpless, quite useless to Elise. He could only lie supinely outside in the water and watch through undimmed eyes what went on.

Then a curtain whisked across the porthole and Dodge was staring at a ghastly pale face, with waving tangled hair, twin headlamps mounted toad-like above the forehead and with glaring, hating, bestial eyes. He recoiled involuntarily, lifting the spear. The face vanished, and Dodge realized that he had very thoroughly frightened himself.

A single shriek pierced the water from the room beyond the curtained window, a single cry cut off sharply.

CHAPTER TWELVE

Coincident with that abruptly stifled cry of: "Jerry!" there came a brittle twang in front of Dodge. A long, stainless steel harpoon grazed the porthole rim, shearing away branches of coral. Dodge whirled. Two men with breathing equipment were diving straight for him. Men with facemasks and respirators and three tanks on their backs, men with harpoon guns, menacing and brutal. Dodge was just a manfish, a pitiful slave, newly risen to pikemanfish status; he laughed at the two clumsy invaders of the underwater realm, flashed past them, twisted, out of their range of vision, and quite callously reached out with the spear and twitched off first one's breather apparatus and then the other's.

He felt nothing as he did this. These were the animals who had captured Elise. These were two less menaces she must face.

He didn't even bother to wait to see them die.

Nothing now must impede his attempt to get inside where he could be of service to Elise. He flew frantically along the wall, seeking for a door, an airlock. After a few moments' frantic search, the very name of what he was seeking brought sanity. *Airlock*. Of what use was an airlock to a man who breathed salt water? To a manfish? To him? He choked on the bitterness of it. Of what use would he be to Elise, bringing in water where she needed air? And, if she seized an aqualung and they escaped from this malodorous coral grotto—what then in the wide immensity of the ocean?

Very well, then. He would go about this some other way. He would be the very acme of brutal overseers, the very pinnacle of filthy overlords. Then—he would deal with that weasel-faced punk. Or, perhaps, it would be better to escape alone? The cold water story had long since been exploded as a myth to fetter new slaves. Escape, find the police, someone—the U.O.P.! And then, with men who could breathe air, come back for Elise. She might be forever denied him; but at least he could return her to the land and the sunshine, away from his ferocious underwater world of darkness and death.

His thoughts were like interplanetary debris, forever chained around a central fact—returned time and again to Elise and her fate. He finned along as fast as he could, angling back into familiar water and streaking for the assembly point.

He arrived just as his sergeant was blowing off steam. Dodge rang his bicycle bell for "All right" showed the spear and signed that he had killed a fire-fish. That mollified the sergeant. The group joined others similarly accoutred and passed into a crevice in the lip of the rim. Below lay the blackness of the deep.

Dodge forced himself to be calm, to obliterate from his mind the searing memory of the last few minutes. Of course, he couldn't. The vision of Elise's face again and again came between him and the lichen-covered walls of the ravine. Three times he almost ran headlong into spreading coral umbrellas. He had to come to grips with himself, with life as it was happening now. He would be of no use to Elise if he wound up a water-logged corpse. Making an effort of will that demanded every spark of courage and determination in him, he shut his fears and terrors and hopes away and concentrated on what he was doing.

For they were heading down into dangerous waters.

There were perhaps fifty menfish in the party. Led by hard-faced sergeants preoccupied with possible double-pronged danger, armed with long spears, twin headlamps giving them a horned, toadlike appearance, shooting with lithe ease and grace downwards in a sinuous line—they ventured into the depths, true representatives of Man, King of the Beasts.

At the first halt on a sandy bottom whose silvery color was washed out already into a spectral gray glimmer, the men formed a half-circle around the group-leader. Dodge knew only that he was called Captain Kitser. His face was seamed and slashed by a lifetime of underwater exploration; his every motion had the fluid grace of a hunting fish. He raised his repeating harpoon for attention and looked deliberately around his command.

"All right. Most of you are new to this game. It's my job to stop you from being killed, and to show you how to kill the enemy. The last, I assure you, is a pleasure."

He adjusted his throat microphone. His voice boomed out, filling the rocky cleft. "I don't know what fantastic stories you've been hearing up there; guff about gigantic sharks and killer whales and I shouldn't wonder. All right! Forget all that! That's the same sort of nonsense as the story about the coldness of the sea. We're down here to do a job. A simple job. A soldier's job."

Dodge had tensed at the blatant mention of the cold. So these men around him were very definitely of the elite-to-be. Either they weren't expected to try to escape anymore, in search of promised rewards from the bosses; or—they were expected to be killed. Dodge gripped his spear rebelliously.

"The company that employs all of us is not a charity institution; we give a day's work and we get a day's life. All right! But other companies don't have the same idea. They send along brigands to steal our equipment, kidnap our workers; even our herds are not safe. All right! We're going to put a stop to that!" He paused and glared around. Dodge reckoned he was putting on quite an act. Most of the men around him, who, until a day ago had been slaves like himself, must before that have been clerks and shop-assistants, traveling salesmen, sports instructors, diving exhibitionists. There were no fishermen in the seas of the world anymore. All the sort of men to be impressed by the curt military command technique. Dodge, though, had been a commander in the Space Force. Until Elise had called him that he'd quite forgotten. His memory

109

and brains were becoming water-logged. Captain Kitser thumped on.

"All right! We have a patrol area. We patrol it. There will be one shark mount for every two men. You will be shown how to control them. And look after them, they are company property. Any man losing a shark will be charged with wilful destruction of company property. All right!"

So he went on, outlining their duties. They were to form a picquet line and spot any raiders, call up the heavies, the tiger-sharks, the fish-drawn artillery, the swordfish cavalry, the subs with their undersea weapons. They would hold the line until the heavies arrived. In any battle that might develop they would be permitted to thrust their spears into the bellies of the enemy; but Captain Kitser really felt that they'd be better occupied getting to hell out of it.

The men agreed—heartily.

Captain Kitser wound up: "You've become accustomed to life in the upper levels over the continental shelf. It's no secret that this particular section is quite shallow. When you dive deeper, into the open sea, you'll meet a far different sort of fish from those you knock about up here. You'll meet sharks that don't turn tail when you put your fingers to your nose! So watch it! You'll draw food and extra power-packs from stores here. There will be a screen of watcher fish and guardians and asdic will be alerted at all times. We hope we spot the raiders before they get in too far. We hope. All right!"

Dodge felt that if he had to ring his bicycle bell for "all right" he'd burst out laughing.

By the time he had fully equipped himself he felt like an Alpine climber. Power pack on back for his heated dress of armored scales. Power packs for the headlamps. The lamps themselves, bulging over his forehead. A food knapsack. Waterbottle. A large wooden-handled bronze bell, with clapper tied down, for use in emergency. His spear. A large searchlight, with immensely thick plastic lens to withstand pressure, equipped with wings and tail. Power packs for the searchlight. All this, plus himself, hanging with a comrade from the sandpapery side of a large dopey shark. The controls were simple. A pair of reins, and a second pair for vertical movement. Dodge took a quick look at the beast's head and saw the tough skin disappear beneath a slightly smoother covering—those damned plastic covers, like the one he had seen lying by that dying mother shark!

Sally came along for the ride.

The men spread out into the water. The blueness was omnipresent now. The familiar scene of the higher levels was gone; there were no comforting lamps studding the floor—there was no floor; only the blackness extending downwards to the pelagic ooze perhaps twelve thousand feet below.

They'd been told that the watcher-fish and the guardians were out there to their front for one very good reason; they effectually prevented escape. Dodge and his companion, a strongly-built, fair-haired Nordic type with blunt, open features and still the remnants of a once-ready smile, who called himself Knut, were carried by their shark along their beat many times. The darkness of the water grew, and Dodge guessed that when the sun set over the surface and the deeps became black and impenetrable and hostile, would be the time for extra vigilance. He was remembering the horror stories of the menfish. Octopus. Barracuda. Electric eels. Killer whales. He might rationalize the credulous belief some men had in these stories and tell himself they were proven fallacies; but it wasn't as easy as that. It was all very stimulating to a manfish patrolling a beat through the cold waters hanging over a twelve thousand foot deep gulf.

Captain Kitser came by, lying on his stomach on a skate. The metal hydrofoil had a store of compressed gas beneath the body, and ejected it through steerable jets from astern. A transparent water-screen curved in front with a powerful gun poking through. The skates were as maneuverable as any fish. Kitser operated the brake and a parachute flared open briefly, halting him in the water, and closing again on springs. He made a quick adjustment to the buoyancy tanks and floated.

"You!" He pointed at Dodge. The light on the skate threw his silhouette up as a monstrous gargoyle. "Back to base. This to Lieutenant Hung Soo. All right!" He thrust over a plastic tube, a message container. With a bubble of gas, the skate skidded on bearing Kitser along the picquet line.

Dodge disengaged from the shark, left Knut there, and flew to base. At the end of the ravine leading down from the edge of a scarp had been built a command post. Here Dodge flew in a round opening, blinking in the lights, and found Lieutenant Hung Soo. He handed over the message and at a sharp command to wait, finned slowly off to a corner, propped himself in the angle of the walls and began to eat a snack. His eyes roved round the command post.

The main item of equipment was the huge radar screen occupying one complete wall. Then Dodge realized that it wouldn't be radar, not undersea. Ultra-sonics, of course. Asdic; or, as some people called it these days, sonar. It was laid out like a radar screen, with concentric circles radiating from a point representing command base. The mass of colored chips of light would be his comrades, the picquet line was quite plain and the restless speck would be Captain Kitser on his skate. Dodge counted heads and stopped when he came to the fleck of light that was his shark and Knut.

The edge of the scarp showed like a coastline. They had the scanner set for a narrow band at approximately the same level, there were no upward and downward sweeps —at least on this board—which would have shown the scattering layer and mysterious shapes lurking in the depths. Dodge wondered, when Kitser's voice came over the sonic speaker, what the message had been about. He saw menfish busily scribbling away at desks and guessed that they were preparing maps or situation appreciations. Certainly, vocal communication was far quicker than a simple soldier's best flying time. Dodge was getting back the feeling of science, of technical marvels, realizing, with a sour thrill, that this was what he had been missing since losing space. The room was full of orderly activity. Come to think of it, it wasn't unlike the bridge of a space cruiser. When action was imminent—and then Dodge saw the action develop, perfectly able to follow it on the screen.

Cheeps of alarm came from speakers set high along the walls. They would be the watcher-fish equipped with echo-sounders. The lines of light on the screen, converging towards command base, developed with indecent swiftness.

The killers were closing in. Excitement gripped Dodge. He could view all this with detachment. It wasn't his battle. Orders were being dispatched over the sonic transmitters. Lieutenant Hung Soo turned to see Dodge, jerked an angry fist, shouted: "Don't worry about the answer, soldier. All hell's breaking loose. Get out there with your spear, fast. We need every man."

Dodge thought: *All right!* and finned away.

A round door, that had been closed when he had passed, was open. Inside he saw rows of menfish busily working at what at first glance appeared to be multibank typewriters. Above were oscillographs with wavering green lines looping ceaselessly. A chittering noise of squeaks and whistles filled the atmosphere, a noise that was like a magnified echo of the noises that sounded all the time in his own ears.

Then a manfish with orange armor prodded a spear across his face and rolled the door shut.

Thinking about that, Dodge flew off towards Knut, his shark and the battle. He never reached them. Gliding out into the mouth of the crevice he had to tread water frantically to allow a battery of fish artillery to thunder by, the fish striving forward with violent lunges, the syringe-shaped cannon streaming behind and fish-mounted men flying all around. Expectantly, he gazed ahead and saw the plastic-cloth banner flaring on the lead fish—guidons into action, yet.

He was tossed up on the wash of water and then, sinking down, again started off, avoiding a two-man sub with externally lashed torpedoes; rounding the bubbling wake he saw Sally go whirling helplessly away in the crush-wave of displaced water. At once he turned and finned hard after her. In a few moments he had caught her; she had vectored up on him, shivering her golden fins, glittering in the light, and they both joined the throngs moving towards the deepening blackness outside. He wouldn't like to lose Sally now.

Somewhere that damned brass band was playing again. This time it was excerpts from "Tannhauser," the "Soldiers' Chorus" and even, so help him, "The British Grenadiers."

Some disc jockey was putting his heart into the struggle.

The lights left to his rear, he turned to parallel the scarp and join up with his section. The throngs in the waters around him, many bearing luridly belching lamps that flicked dramatically over limbs and flippers, and shot shards of light from weapons and armor, spread out away from the scarp face. He had a vivid impression of a steel foundry at night. He decided to stick to the picquet line and find Knut, and soon he was flying through dark areas of insufficient light, with an oddly lumpy feeling in his stomach he could not at first identify.

Away out to his right fire-fly lights were flickering uncertainly; if that was the watcher-fish line then it was being pushed in pretty deeply. Dodge rebelled against this underwater incarceration in the moment he recognized the lumpiness in his stomach was fear, nerve-constricting, muscle-paralyzing fear; he had a fierce desire for this fight to be over, for him to be free to get back to the farm and see what he could do to rescue Elise.

Menfish straggled past him, going from right to left. In an odd patch of light from a drifting globe he saw blood staining the water. It floated like sooty clouds. A crazy shark swept past, half its tail missing, its guts trailing. A dead manfish bobbed with mouth open and eyes glassy, gradually sinking. He had twelve thousand feet to fall before he would be buried.

Dodge began to feel really panicky. He quelled that before it reached his higher brain centers, and tried to think things out. The water was quite dark now. Emerald green lights here and there, all the more magnificent for the emphasis of inky blackness between, gave erratic, fragmentary illumination. Visibility was down to a hand's-breadth. Shouts and screams came clearly through the water. Dodge periodically turned on his back and checked the area to his rear. A line of menfish, their armor torn and blood drifting away, went finning madly past him. He saw a floating syringe cannon drifting sluggishly.

Sally was worried. She kept darting away and then fluttering back. Dodge could almost sense her near hysteria.

He heard a dull concussion. He saw nothing, but the next instant a gigantic padded fist had thumped him in the chest. He gasped, retching. His ears ached. Somewhere a sub had exploded.

More menfish straggled past, their lights a weaving uncertain pattern of panicky will-o'-the-wisps. Armor glinted. So the soldiers, too, had been beaten. Time to turn back. He was not at all surprised when Harp flew up, spotted Dodge and curved back. This, he had been expecting with one segment of his brain. Harp's arm was gashed, the bloody bandage of little use surrounded by sea water.

Dodge thrust his spear forward, baring his teeth. When he couldn't say what he felt, that was as good a way as any of showing what he thought of Harp. Harp smiled weakly. His throat worked convulsively; Dodge heard the swallow over the amplifier.

"I guess you feel sore, Jerry. I'll tell you all about it later. Had to do it, for all our sakes. Tried to tip you off things weren't what they seemed by calling my harpoon a spear." He raised the harpoon, pointed. "Now we'll have to get the hell outta here. There's something out there that's mighty bad medicine. Yes sir."

And, again, Dodge wasn't surprised that he believed Harp. The business with the spear and harpoon hadn't meant a thing to him at the time; he'd been in no condition for fine, fancy semantics. He nodded, once, and pulled the spear back.

A fish swam quickly into the lighted area from their headlamps. A long, slender fish, perhaps seven feet from snout to tail. It reminded Dodge of a Zeppelin. The mouth curved down, the chin raked forward like a battleship's ram and the eyes were round and large. It hung, poised, and half opened its mouth. Dodge saw the teeth, needle sharp, long—the mouth was a wedge of jutting ferocity.

Harp aimed his harpoon and sent the shaft directly into the fish's head. Then he turned and began working his flippers like a madman. Frightened, Dodge followed.

The fish had been something deadly. He had never seen its like undersea before; the long, slender silhouette, with the classic grace of the perfect underwater form, created an impression on the mind that could never be erased. He caught up with Harp. Harp glanced round and went on finning.

His words were chopped, short, brutal. "Barracuda. Hundreds of 'em. Coming in in droves. Being beaten in as a screen for the raiders. Blood mad, all of 'em. Gotta get back to command post."

Dodge realized at once that this was the opportunity for escape. The whole undersea farm was in turmoil. All authority and control had been torn to shreds. He could fly away now, unwounded, rise up to the higher levels, get clear off. The barracuda would follow the wounded men-fish into the ravine for the final struggle.

He looked upwards. There lay freedom.

Then he remembered. Harp with a wounded arm trailing blood and a long haul to command post. Elise, penned in that prison. Ironical—escape under those circumstances. He tried to think clearly, to make the right decision.

Sally swam frantically past him, went streaking ahead.

A long, slender shape followed. The barracuda aroused a choking feeling of utter revulsion in Dodge. All that beauty of form allied with the insensate ferocity of that expression—those teeth—

He looked around. Harp's blood stained the water. He couldn't leave him now.

In the murky light from a drifting globe he saw the sea behind him brimming with the darting shapes of barracuda.

The sea boiled.

No use thinking of Elise now, or of Harp, or Sally. No use thinking of escape. No use thinking of anything . . .

CHAPTER THIRTEEN

The results of the debate on the "Under Ocean Phenomena of an Inimicable Nature" had been catastrophic. By a small majority, the Assembly and the Security Council had voted to drop an atomic bomb on Juliana Trench.

Simon Hardy was livid. Henderson was tensed and nervous. Minister of Aquiculture Werner could talk of nothing but the danger to his crop and herds.

In the turmoil following Henderson's announcement of the possibility of intelligent life of an extra-terrestrial nature in the Juliana Trench and the absolute chaos, shattering coherent thought, consequent on the UN decision to drop a "small" atomic bomb, a "punitive" atomic bomb, Captain Pinhorn of the Space Force and his queries about a certain missing Space Force commander had been brusquely brushed aside. Pinhorn raged; but raged vainly. "Wait until Mr. Grosvenor gets here," he had been told. And when Grosvenor had arrived, and been questioned, he had said that he didn't know where young Dodge was, and he had added testily that he'd also like to know what had happened to Miss Tarrant, who was an efficient secretary and good secretaries were difficult to find these days, what with all the girls chasing off to go sea-larking about under the water . . .

A fast trip by submarine—quicker than by strato-jet as he was able to decompress during the voyage—to the Blue Deep Hotel was just a waste of time. Pinhorn had learned, though, that a young Siamese girl and her brother had vanished at the same time as Dodge and Miss Tarrant. Apart from that, everyone said, going back to their harpoons and flippers and making for the airlocks and the husky young instructors, they didn't know a thing. Pinhorn fumed.

The Ocean triumvirate—Henderson, Hardy and Werner —did all they could to reverse the UN atomic bomb decision.

They lobbied and pleaded, threatened and bribed, quoted sea pollution, destruction of food-stuffs—all in vain.

"If," said Dahlak Major, UN General Secretary, "you weren't worried about these monsters under the sea, you wouldn't have brought the subject up in Assembly. They'll be dealt with, the seas made safe for your exploration, and everyone's happy." Dahlak Major smiled complacently. He was a tough, resilient, constructive type of man who knew that the less corns you stepped on in world affairs the better you'd integrate help when help was needed; but who was well aware, too, that if corns had to be trodden on they should be squashed flat, without argument—preferably with the help of someone bigger than the squashee.

"This decision has not been taken lightly, Admiral Hardy," he said carefully. "We don't make a habit of tossing atomic bombs around. But the situation is perfectly clear. The seas must be made safe for humanity."

"But that's not the point!" Hardy answered from Trident. "We want to go down there as friends. If they have an atomic bomb dropped on them, and they're really some sort of people from another star system, then what will they do next? It's like stirring up a grouper with your little finger. If you're going to drop anything on them," he said wrathfully, intending to ridicule the idea in the clear light of reason, "why play around cheap-skate stuff with an atomic bomb? You'd much better drop a hydrogen bomb on them and do the job up proud!" His voice was loaded with sarcasm.

Dahlak said, "Okay, Admiral Hardy. If you want a hydrogen bomb dropped, an H-bomb it will be. Settled." His tones conveyed the impression that he was not the sort of person who relishes being ridiculed.

When Hardy got through cursing his big mouth, Henderson waded in. Nothing could convince the Security Council that this was not a grave threat to the security of Earth. The Space Force was solidly behind the decision. As Dahlak put it: "Man is reaching out to the stars. Pretty soon we'll be on the satellites of Saturn." Here Toxter of the Space Board nodded complacently. "So we just cannot have any extra-terrestrial race stabbing us in the back from our own door-step." Hardy and Henderson knew what he meant, all right, however garbled his way of saying it. "We are the masters of our own planet—all of it. Including the seas. No monsters from other planets are going to start taking those over. No sirree."

So that was that. The Air Corps Department of the Defence Forces took over and readied a ten-jet bomber. The plane was an anachronism, anyway, and they had to get it out of mothballs and that took time.

Meanwhile, Captain Pinhorn reported to the Moon that he was getting precisely nowhere, and suggested that pressure be brought to bear on Toxter to bear down on Henderson. That idea was negated. No one had any other thoughts at the present time than the H-bomb that was going to be dropped on those terrible deep-sea monsters—all eyes, my dear, shuddery!—with the nerve to come and set up house in Earth's own seas.

Pinhorn requested and received permission to carry out private work on the case, and at once went into closed session with Pierre Ferenc. By the time their party broke up—with an empty whisky bottle to show for it—they knew exactly what they were going to do. Whether it would be any good, neither of them knew.

Hardy had seized this opportunity to press for a drastic increase in his personnel strength—and had won. Jubilantly, in some small way partially compensated for the stupendous blunder in dropping an H-bomb, he planned to clean up the Bishop Wilkins farms. He was looking forward to that work. And, for the hell of it, and as Grosvenor was still down in Trident, he'd start with the Artful Dodger's lot.

When he called for his aide, Pierre Ferenc, though, he was told that—under orders from him—Ferenc and Captain Pinhorn had taken off in a sub, with all manner of supplies, headed for an undisclosed destination.

Hardy started cussing—and then a gleam came into his peculiar eyes. He smiled.

"Young rips. Off after that Dodge, I'll bet. Well, good luck to 'em. As for Pierre—I'll have a most unpleasant quarter of an hour with that young man when he gets back—if he does," he added, suddenly thoughtful.

The sea boiled.

A ghostly glimmering sheen lit around his thrashing fins. Hundreds of tiny Noctilucae, sparking as they were jolted, formed a shimmering train to his frantically laboring body. Dodge had never been more frightened in his life. As never before he was conscious of his surroundings; the immense depth of water around him, and insubstantiality of everything, nothing still, nothing onto which he could grip and hold. He felt suffocated, crushed, panic stricken.

Sweeping in from the open sea hundreds of swarming torpedo-shaped bodies flashed and blazed with their trails of Noctilucae creating an unprecedented display. Surging in with bloody-hungry, stimulated lust, thousands of barracuda tore into the pitifully weak and fleeing men and sharks and terrified fish tamed by men. The rout was complete. In the darkness only the occasional dimly glimmering glow of a lamp, lighting up the waters momentarily with a greenish luster, or the summer lightning of the fire-lit Noctilucae, served to show for an instant the terror and drama being enacted in the deep.

Dodge and Harp flew with agonized speed, expecting each moment to feel the grip of great jaws around their feet, or, in the last expiring fragment of life, to feel their sides torn away. The suspense, just pumping madly with his flippers and thrashing with his arms—against all common-sense—almost unnerved Dodge. When he saw in the instant before collision the great body before him, saw Harp reel back from the blow, he knew that they were lost.

Something hung there in the darkness off the rim, something dead and silent. Dodge thrust desperately to fly around it. Something protruded from it, something hard. His spear rang on metal. He stared, too shocked to think.

It was a sub. A two man sub. Drifting, lightless, dead. Now he could feel the current which had dragged it here pulling at his body. Harp swung around. His headlamps blazed up. Their dumb-bell glare glowed on metal hull, elevators, conning-tower, periscopes, a flung-open hatch.

Harp flicked himself up. Dodge followed, his heart struggling to thrust his viscid blood around his body.

The sub was empty.

Harp went in head first. As Dodge poised to dive in he was for an instant conscious of the sea pressing around him as a living, hating, implacable enemy.

Even as he went headfirst into the sub he felt a tremendous blow on his right leg. His calf hit the side of the conning tower and immediately his leg went numb.

He fell down on top of Harp. His senses were completely disoriented. He felt arms reach past him. There came the muffled hissing-thud of the gas harpoon. His ears sang. Then Harp had reached up, thrusting with Dodge's spear, forced the barracuda out and pulled down the lid. Absolute darkness engulfed them.

At once a terrible panic assailed Dodge. Had anything else crawled or swam or slithered into the sub before they had found it? Were there voracious man-eaters even now stealing upon him from the darkness? He could not scream out. He tried to. His throat muscles jumped and strained with the effort.

Something touched him. His head cracked against the overhead in automatic response. He nearly blacked out.

Harp said: "That was a near go, Jerry, old son. We only just made it."

Dodge sagged. He could feel Harp's fingers on his arm. He could not reply, anyway; if he'd been standing in the cool crisp air of a summer evening in an English garden, he could not have spoken to save his life.

"Put your lights on, Jerry. Yanked the flex out of mine squirming about in that manhole up there."

As he switched on his headlights with trembling fingers, without the strength left to curse himself for forgetting them, Dodge was remembering that other manhole through which he had fallen. That had been the beginning of a nightmare. This time it was the beginning of life.

They were in an enclosed space filled with machinery, controls, dials and meters, thick tubes and trunk pipes leading everywhere. Harp pushed the butt end of a tube upwards; Dodge guessed it was the periscope, although from where he was jammed against the overhead, he couldn't see the eyepiece. He became aware that Dodge was staring at something below his feet. He glanced down.

His right flipper had been chopped off cleanly an inch from his foot. The plastic looked as though it had been perforated and then torn along the holes. He knew where the rest of the fin was. In that barracuda's mouth.

He clung to the overhead, feeling sick.

His leg was still numb. The rest of his body was at once on fire and deathly cold. He shivered. Harp pursed his lips.

"Hold on, Jerry. Reckon this sub came along right on time." Dodge wanted to say something; but he felt too weak to carry out the pantomime of forming words. Harp went on: "I don't think there's much point our going back to the command post now. Don't think much of it will be left."

After his experiences, Dodge couldn't agree more. He wedged himself more comfortably against the lattice-work of tubes and struts against the bulkhead, and made little effort to fight the fatigue that broke over him. There was an unfinished task to be seen to, something in which he believed with undiminished vigor; but right now it was easier to lie up here against the metal and watch Harp creeping about in the glow of the lamps.

Harp said quietly: "Look down here, Jerry."

Dodge moved his head down. The dumb-bell shape of light from his twin headlamps flicked across the metal walls and piping, jumped the angle of walls and deck, centered on Harp's feet. The harpooner was standing on the deck, an opened locker door held up with one hand; with the other he extended a throat microphone and amplifier set. "Lucky find, Jerry. Thought there'd be a spare around. Now you can tell me what you think of me for calling you a slavey."

As Dodge took the set, roused and stimulated in a

frighteningly minor way, he smiled wryly. So Harp hadn't forgotten either! He adjusted the equipment, coughed and swallowed and heard the gulp echo in the sub's control room. Then he said: "All right!" He laughed, weakly.

"You all right, Jerry?"

"Yes. Those barracuda—scared the living daylights out of me." It was communication again; he was speaking; he had returned to the articulate world, his dumbness had barred him from for so long. The way he was feeling it didn't, really, seem to matter.

"Me too," Harp paused, and Dodge sensed the awkwardness behind the next words. "Look, old son, I had to play it tough that day. I'd just been accepted into the guards, they thought I was a good-boy, willing to play it along their way and I was scared someone might spill the beans on me. I planned to get you and Elise and Lura out . . ."

"How did you think you could do that?"

"It wouldn't have been easy. I found out where the girls were hidden—funny I should go for that Siamese dame like that, guess I just don't know my own tastes —but there were always air-breathing guards about." He relished his scorn. "Clumsy, bumbling gas-tanks! Still, they were too strong to be knocked off, and, anyway, getting the girls out from the rest of the harem would have been a . . ."

"Harem!"

"Well, what did you think they wanted those girls for? Waitresses in the officers' mess?" He sounded bitter. "I don't know what happened to Lura and Elise; never got a chance to speak to them; but as soon as I'd found you I began to put the plan into operation." Harp spoke in a level monotone; it was evident that all his emotion had drained out long ago; his fears for the Siamese girl must have tempered his spirit into a single desire to atone.

Dodge was expected to say: "What plan?" Instead, he said: "I had a chat with Elise; just before I got out here. Up to that time she and Lura were okay. But they were having a bust-up with a rat-faced punk as I left—I heard someone scream 'Jerry!'—and, well . . ."

"You talked to them!"

Dodge explained. Harp said quickly: "That weasel-faced animal is Danny Agostini. Personal bodyguard to the boss. No one ever sees him, of course. He was the rat who took us in the sub. You remember, when we got out of that sub-tow balloon."

"I remember. That seems like years ago."

Through the metal hull rang thumps from the outside world, a curious blend of dull thud and abrupt ringing. "Cuda," Harp said laconically.

"What do you plan to do now?"

"Well, the whole situation's changed, to put it originally. I was all for blasting in, knocking off the guards, getting the girls and heading for the surface. We'd have made it, too."

"Perhaps. But right now?"

Harp gestured round the sub as more ominous sounds battered outside. "I've a fair idea on running these things. They're designed to be operated by menfish, and this one obviously had the crew knocked off by the raiders. It drifted with that current that sets in along number four turbine generator . . ."

"I know it," murmured Dodge.

"—and if we can, then there's nothing to stop us from using it to get the girls out. They should be safe enough for the night in that undersea palace you were talking about. But I'm not going outside here until daylight. Cuda —I hate 'em! So—you're going to dress this scratch, I'm going to eat and then sleep. Check?"

It was aggravating; but it was logical and the only way. Dodge, summoning all his reserves, smiled, and said: "All right!"

"So you met gallant Captain Kitser, too, huh. Wonder what he's doing now?"

Which was not the pleasantest of thoughts.

After they had eaten and Harp's wound had been dressed from the first aid locker, and just as they were twisting to find reasonably comfortable positions, and fighting not to think too much about their decision and what it might mean to Elise and Lura, Dodge remembered something. He swore tiredly.

"Damn! I lost Sally!"

CHAPTER FOURTEEN

Far to the north the mighty herds were driven across the ranches of the ocean, coralled, counted, calves branded and the annual toll taken. The people of the dry land took the sacrifice of the whales, and used it, each in his different way, and spared a casual glance for the annual reports of tonnages and heads in the financial columns. Across the wide ranges of the open sea the shoals of fish moved like endless rivers of flesh, driven by electrical currents that guided them through their spinal columns without the fish's own volition. Subs checked their flanks, fish-mounted outriders patrolled ceaselessly; but inevitably the sea was stained its muddy brown, the blood of a million fish that could not yet be adequately protected against the killers of the sea. Not yet had Man tamed his planet, not yet had he imprinted the orderly pattern of his husbandry upon all the creatures of the ocean.

Somewhere in that immensity of rolling water two men sat in a small sub. One man stared stupefiedly at the other, who laughed and laughed and breathed exaggeratedly in and allowed the water to flow luxuriously from his gill slits.

Captain Pinhorn said incredulously: "But you can't! You can't breathe under water!"

Pierre Ferenc did just that, and said: "I'm sorry. I thought you knew."

He'd at last grown so weary of sitting in the air-filled sub, breathing through the deep-sea mask, that he'd abruptly told Pinhorn to watch it and had flooded the sub. Pinhorn was wearing one of the three-tank sets—two of helium and one of oxygen, with a demand regulator set to strangle the supply of oxygen with the increase in pressure; so that at extreme depths no more pressurized oxygen was coming through with the helium than was necessary, and therefore oxygen poisoning, fatal at nine atmospheres unless you were quick and got out of it, could not attack. The two men guided the sub cautiously towards the Arthur Dodge Wilkins Corporation, watching their asdic, checking their position, until at last they came floating into the shambles.

When they had covered most of the headquarters area, Ferenc sent back an ultra-sonic message to Trident. It was terse. Whoever had wrought this destruction must have the mentality of a maniac. A few barracuda haunted the scene and Ferenc harpooned one and hauled it aboard. As he studied it, his eyes went narrow and his mouth turned as mean as the dead beast under his fingers.

When daylight at last seeped through the watery strata, bringing back to life that mysterious blue world of the undersea, Dodge and Harp stared eagerly from the port.

"If we were still in the current, we should be over the farms now."

Outside there was blueness, stretching away on all sides and upwards; below was deep and impenetrable blackness.

"Well, that's that, then. We're lost."

"Lost! But that's impossible!" protested Dodge. "We can drive this thing, you say. There must be maps, charts. We can use the asdic . . ."

"Sure I can drive this sub. But can you figure out our position? Do you know where the farms were? Can you tell me which way to go?"

Dodge looked numb. Savagely he began to eat. There was plenty of food in the lockers, together with a supply of drinking water, which they took through a non-return valve spout. Just like space, Dodge said. Only—the trick was to jam the cupped end of the spout into the mouth against the palate, cutting off entry of salt. When the meal

126

was over, Harp said: "Think I'll take a look at the engines. Down that hatch." He pointed to the deck.

Dodge was leaning against the forward screen, idly tapping the metal rim. He glanced miserably at Harp as the hatch cover came up. Harp flopped over onto his stomach and put his head down. He jerked up. His arm came back and in his fist was a man's hair. He hauled.

The engineer had been a fat manfish. There was little left on his bones now; just enough to show that he had been plump and well fed. Dodge was just beginning to feel ill, nauseated at having slept with that—that thing—down there all night, when Harp shouted in a high, shocked voice.

In a smooth flurry of flippers he edged back. Over his armored shoulders Dodge saw the round eye, the pointed snout quite unlike a shark's, the suddenly gaping head with the chin more prominent than the nose and rows of needle-like teeth. He watched petrified. His hand stretched out at last, breaking the spell, out towards his spear.

Harp suddenly shouted violently, beat his hands up and down, thrashed in the water. According to the rules that should have scared off anything, including barracuda.

The fish did not budge. It flicked its tail. Dodge knew it was going to hurl itself forward at an impossible speed, going to take Harp's head off in one gargantuan bite. Everything happened as though frozen. His fingers gripped the spear. With his useless right flipper he could not balance properly—he twisted his body with muscle-punishing speed and hurled the spear. The point penetrated the eye of the cuda just as it hurled itself forward.

Harp rolled away. His fist took the pantherish body under the gills. The cuda, the spear standing out like a pig-sticker, rolled, trailing blood. The blow sent it clean over Harp's head. Then the square harpooner had his harpoon, and had sent with blurring rapidity, three arrows to splatter into the big, beautiful body. He was shaking all over. His convulsive swallowings crashed in the cabin.

"Damn cuda!" He lashed out with a flipper and tipped the streamlined body over. It wasn't dead yet; the tail moved spasmodically and the mouth yawned.

Then Harp had darted forward and was peering at the massive, ugly head. Dodge joined him to stare down. In

127

the head, solitary, enigmatic, a single metal needle stuck up like a lone pin in a pin-cushion.

"See that!" Harp said sharply.

"Like that dying mother shark." Dodge told Harp about her and his acquisition of Sally, now vanished, as the harpooner worked away at the needle. When it was out they saw that it was an electrode, hair-fine—some of it had snapped off in the tiny brain beneath—and the thicker exterior part contained a minute electrical battery that had, they found by experiment on their skin, long lost its power.

"My ideas on that begin to add up," Dodge said slowly. "Electrodes in brains—in particular areas of brain. Harp, that poor damn fish had an electrical stimulus applied to a certain center of its brain! And it doesn't take two guesses to know which part!" He was gripped with wonder and horror at this discovery. "The pain center! That fish was under the compulsive of continuous pain stimulation. No wonder those barracuda were raving mad!"

"I've heard about that. Experiments on rats."

"Yes. Apply an electrical shock to a pleasure center and let the rat find the lever to touch to operate it, and the hedonistic animal will go on giving himself pleasure shocks until he's exhausted. Then radio-control. Animals responding to directions piped straight from electrical batterings into their brains. And now some devils have translated that to fish. No wonder the fish are under such absolute control. That shark I saw had a nettle-field of needles. They must have been able to play tunes with her . . ." He stopped talking abruptly. He put a hand to his forehead, rubbed his temples with finger and thumb. "When I was in that command post," he said, "I saw a row of menfish operating boards of keys with screens in front of them. They were controlling the fish! By ultra-sonics! It's easy! Of course, that's the way they do it."

"Training. Black and white, yes-no," elaborated Harp. "Indoctrinate the fish with simple commands. More complex orders can be beamed out. Press this stud, the fish gets a jolt of juice in the pain center. Press this stud, his fins flick left; release the pain—presto—he's going where you want him!"

"That's about the size of it," said Dodge.

"In time you'd have a set pattern of conditioned re-flexes. They wouldn't control every minute movement from base . . ." Harp bent as he was talking and began to remove the dead manfish's flippers. "They'd leave that to those operators on the two-man sleds. They always seemed to be loaded with electronic gear. They could have got those fish to jump through hoops for them."

They disposed of the dead engineer through the hatch; but Dodge insisted that they hang the barracuda and the electrode buried in its brain in a store cupboard. Harp checked the engines, and reported gloomily that they were beyond immediate repair. As the light increased in the waters beyond the port, throwing a shimmering blue luster on all the metal surfaces, and stroking pale fingers of vagrant pearl along the bodies and limbs of the menfish, Dodge and Harp tried, with waning hope, to control and guide the sub. Harp, at length, looked through the port and turned back to Dodge to say: "Well, old son. According to the rules, you and I should be due for the poisons tank."

"What's that?"

"We're in an up-current. Must have been swept across the farms during the night and now we're heading God knows where. But the water is definitely lightening."

And so it was.

Later on that day, when even the approach of evening had not brought its customary early pall into the depths, and the water still showed long blue reaches, they had resigned themselves to drifting indefinitely under the sur-face. It was an odd, transient mood, and one which Dodge felt would soon pass, leaving them free to plan for the future. The first intimation they had that they were no longer alone came when three peremptory raps re-sounded on the hull. They exchanged baffled looks.

"If they've caught up with us," Harp growled, "I feel sorry for the first seven." He fondled his magnum harpoon.

Dodge had pulled out a repeater harpoon and Harp had told him how to use it. There were twenty-five sharp slivers of stainless steel with hollow poison heads. They waited whilst the knocking was repeated. Through the port they caught a glimpse of a rapidly finning leg, an arm with bracelets encircling it, a tapering-fingered hand grasping a repeater harpoon. A face pressed against the transparent plastic. A face with a green hair and wide eyes, curved, impudent mouth and even, pale-blue teeth. Dodge flung his headlights on; the beam showed momentarily in a patch of plankton and the face outside brightened into its true colors. Fair hair, crisp white teeth and smiling red lips.

She knocked again, the recognized signal for "Open up!"

"Okay," said Dodge. "Let her in."

Two small bodies flashed in, began gesticulating, forming words, cavorting about. "Give her the amplifier," said Dodge. He did not tell her that it had just been taken from the throat of a manfish ripped apart by barracuda, although, oddly enough, he felt the news would not have inconvenienced her. She looked ruggedly independent, like the youngster with her.

When the throat mike and amplifier were adjusted, she said: "I'm Pawnee. This is my brother Cuth. That's short for Cuthbert"—she avoided a violent kick from her brother's flipper—"and he hates the name. Welcome to Neptunia."

"If you're welcoming us to the sea," Dodge said harshly, "that's superfluous. What is Neptunia? Who are you?"

She laughed unselfconsciously. "Neptunia is rather corny, I suppose, but when Gramps and his gang found it, it must have sounded very grand. And they had a struggle to keep it going at all in the early years."

Bit by bit, interspersed by violent altercations carried on between Pawnee and Cuth in rapid, bewildering, sign language, the story came out. It was essentially a simple story, an inevitable one, given the set-up of the slave labor on underwater farms, and the ease of life in the oceans to people who knew how to cope with the alien environment.

"Only it isn't an alien environment at all," said Pawnee, shaking her head so that the strands of her fair hair waved like undersea fronds. "If you know your way around it's a lot more comfortable than trying to live in 'cities'. Whatever they are. And fancy trying to fly upright on your flippers and move by putting one in front of the other and falling on it!" She and Cuth giggled.

"I'd like a quick walk through the Strand into Trafalgar Square and the Park right now," Dodge said sharply. The brother and sister regarded him quickly, then their hands blurred in speech. Pawnee said, shyly: "You want to leave the sea?"

"Leave it? I'd like to boil the lot away!"

Her gasp of horror sobered Dodge. Quite illogically, he felt guilty, as though he had just said something abominable, something unforgivable. He flicked a flipper up and began to massage his calf where it still felt numb. So he might be in the wrong; but he couldn't apologize. It was difficult enough trying to keep a perspective on life down here under the water without telling lies about how much he liked it. He yearned, abruptly, tearingly, for the clean sweep of the stars. And, absurdly coupled in with that grand romantic notion was the itchy feeling that he'd like to feel the tingle of a good clean soap-and-water wash.

Neptunia, they discovered, was a drowned ocean peak. Within its rocky crevices and fastnesses, and on its multiplicity of terraces extending downward into utter blackness, lived a large and continually shifting population. Originating when a group of escaped slaves had clung fainting to it in the midst of the ocean, it had grown from their need to live, into a proliferating colony of active and independent vitality. Running under a vague and ill-defined form of anarchy, with a few of the elder men putting in an odd word or two of advice, it had formed the lode-stone to which all escaped menfish in this area of the seas were ultimately drawn. Most reached it by the same method that had brought Dodge and Harp; the strong, mellow sweep of the ocean currents. In those currents, too, came all manner of debris, wrecks, food and flotsam and jetsam. The culture was not poor.

"And you say you were born here?" asked Dodge when at last they stood on the rocky jetty, ninety feet below the surface. Old-fashioned xenon arc-lamps blazed down, their undersea river turbines barely able to generate enough power to force light from the tungsten electrodes through ten feet of water. Lower down, said Pawnee, there were more modern lamps. She turned her head, her hair rising like the sweep of an anemone.

"Of course we were born here. Birth under the sea is

quite the norm—sharks are ovoviparous, aren't they? And rays and sword-tails? And sea-water is probably, being like blood, a better place to have a child in than air . . ."

"All right," said Dodge, failing to smile. "But Lamarckism doesn't apply to sexually reproducing animals. How come you were born into a water-breathing world, when a million years or so of evolution have fitted you to breathe air?"

"Silly. As soon as young are born they are placed in airspaces and operated on by waldoes manipulated by some of the best surgeons in the sea. It's a process that follows naturally, and then the babies are given back to their mothers."

"Hum," said Dodge intelligently.

They finned through a chamber where Pawnee's father greeted them. Escaped slaves these people might have been, living perennially in the sea; but they had a vitality, an aliveness, and awareness of living, that had been completely missing from Dodge's experience since he had first ventured underwater. With something of a shock he realized that he hadn't been above the surface since first going through the airlock in the Blue Deep Hotel with Elise. That jolted his memory.

"We came here on a current—you probably know it very well. We're anxious to find our way back to the Bishop Wilkins farm. Can you help us?"

"You tell them, Pops," said Pawnee, doubtfully.

"It isn't easy." Pawnee's father might have been the merry old sea monarch King Neptune himself. "There are any number of different streams converging south of here, flowing up towards the north. Gulf Stream material. The thing is, there is a lot of unrest in the sea. Comings and goings. Messages have come in that the fish are in turmoil. Clearing out. Masses of barracuda have been sighted . . ."

"You don't have to tell us, Pop," said Harp. He explained. "But we have to try to get back."

"I'll talk it over with some of the others. Of course, we'll try to help; but we are without so-called law and order here. If you can't pay for help, well—it may be a little difficult."

"We've got the sub we came in," Dodge said hotly.

"Under your rules I suppose that's ours, now? Well, just give us the directions and a little time to refit, and we'll be off."

Cuth, floating slowly down the ceiling, said: "How do we know you're not blasted farm spies?"

That, like a douche of fresh water, put everything in a cold, new perspective. Cuth hung there, moving his flippers lightly, watching them.

Surprisingly enough, as Dodge was spluttering out some garbled denial, Pop said: "I don't think they are, son. I've told you I don't know how many times that the farms know about us, a little, anyway; they leave us alone, now. The cost of any expedition against us would be prohibitive."

"Now," said Pawnee. "What about later?"

The voices were muffled and thick, but clearly audible, and Dodge and Harp disconnected their amplifiers. They were near the surface, and thought of that quickened Dodge's pulse. He could appreciate this community's fears of raids from the Corporations and guessed that they would be a very tough nut to crack—this was their home. A blue-gray blur like a yo-yo shot across the chamber three feet off the floor. It halted with a swirl of arms, hunched up, and dropped on Pawnee's shoulder. Two globular eyes regarded Dodge impassively.

Involuntarily, he recoiled. An octopus! Pawnee put up a hand and pulled a tentacle, then tut-tutted and carefully readjusted an orange bow around the upper section of tentacle. The octopus stretched its legs languorously. It was a good four feet across.

"Some pet," said Dodge.

In his ears always, now, was that singing undercurrent of tantalizing sound which defied recognition. It rose and fell, altering with events, enigmatic, infuriating.

Over a magnificent meal, matters were thrashed out. Pop felt secure in Neptunia. He was happy with the system—or lack of it—by which the colony functioned; it was efficient, which was what mattered. He was the acknowledged leader in any time of stress and with his beard and heavy, cheerful features so like the imagined Sea Monarch of legend, he carried the position off faultlessly. Dodge, rubbing his own smooth cheeks where depilatories applied years before had effectively prevented any further hair growth, wondered how Pop had got on with a facemask before his elevation to the status of man-fish. Pop knew there were other outlaw nests in the seas, it was the inevitable corollary of any unstable culture like slave-states. The barracuda presented a baffling mystery. No one thought that any Bishop Wilkins farm would be maniacal enough to employ such a drastic method of raiding a rival concern. Dodge considered this, chewing a ham-tasting fish-bone, and was forced to agree. From the little he had seen of the underwater realm, he knew that profits and food production should go hand in hand; destroying a rival didn't help you much. Apart from not gaining any slaves, the rival's patents were still good for his land and sea areas—and you wanted live menfish as slaves, not bloating—if menfish did bloat—corpses.

But Pop was adamant that the other outlaw nests wouldn't think of employing such a barbaric method of warfare; Neptunia wouldn't—so why should they? Dodge wished he could be so sure. Anyway, Pop had pointed out, Neptunia was the nearest slave refuge in these seas, wasn't it? So why should anyone else come bursting in poaching their sea?

Sometime during the meal, Harp said: "Don't you want to leave here? Get back to civilization?"

The answer was painfully obvious.

"Why should we?" Cuth said indifferently. "We like it here. Freedom, plenty of fun, a spot of work now and again, sport—you should have seen that Marlin I tagged the other day!"

"I should have thought you'd hated your parents who took away your birthright. To live on the land. To see the stars . . ."

"But we do see them," Pawnee interjected. "On a dark night up near the surface, the stars are quite plain. And there's always a rainbow round the Moon."

"A rainbow round the Moon," said Dodge. He pushed his plate away; it skidded, and rose into the water, gliding down surrounded by a squirming mass of brilliant tiny fish. "I wonder if I'll ever see her again?"

"Come up tonight, Jerry," said Cuth. "Moon's due, judging by the tides . . ."

"I meant, son, whether I'd ever go up there again."

That precipitated an avalanche. Dodge spent most of the next few hours talking. His throat couldn't become dry, but his muscles ached all along his neck. The kids were insatiable. Eventually, Pop interrupted and packed them off, full of garbled information about life on the Moon, Mars, Venus and Mercury. Dodge had just been getting around to the Jovian satellites. He flopped back, smiling.

"They'll make good spacemen yet," he said. "Could do with a few well-trained menfish on Venus."

"What are we going to do?" Harp said impatiently. He looked thoughtfully at Dodge. "And you never said you were in the Space Force, Jerry. Your pals will be looking for you."

Dodge sat up, finning to stop himself rising. "I'd never thought of that! Good Lord! You're right!"

"So?"

"Well. We get the sub mended, find out the directions and high-tail it back to the farm. Elise and Lura have just got to be all right." He reached for his harpoon. "After that we break for the surface . . ."

"And then what?"

"I know, I know." Dodge slammed the harpoon down angrily. "Air and water don't mix."

"Why not come back here? We don't have much choice, do we? Pop says that none of the slaves he's ever known have ever been able to breathe air again. They all talk about it, get promised the cure as a reward; but no one ever actually gets the surgery. If there is any surgery."

Dodge didn't know whether to admire or dislike what he saw on Harp's face. He brushed a drifting cloud of plankton that had squeezed through the filters somehow aside, and tried to make up his mind. Harp knew what he was giving up; the convincing argument was that they couldn't live on the surface again. They must stay in the depths for the rest of their lives. Life here was just about bearable, he supposed. Hunting for food—no one need starve. The ever-flowing spring of fresh water within the sunken atoll took care of drink. Tinkering with bits of wreck. Growing old. Raising kids.

A life.

He narrowed his eyes on Harp. Harp looked uncomfortable.

"So you'd bring Lura here, have the surgeons operate, turn her into a girlfish, a mermaid, just for your sake?"

"No! Not my sake. We got along well in the sub-tow balloon. I love her, Jerry, crazy though that may be. She'd come. If I asked her to, she'd come."

She would, too. Dodge knew that. It was something of the way he felt about Elise. But he hadn't the courage, or the faith, to ask her what Harp was prepared to ask Lura.

In the days that followed Dodge found that what Harp proposed to ask Lura was not so irrevocably final a negation of life as he had supposed. It was surprising and heart-warming to discover the level of culture there could be under the sea. The contrast between the happy, carefree, almost pagan way of life in Neptunia and the grim, ponderous crushing of life and spirit in the farms forced a sword of pain into his guts.

Music was playing nearly all the time in various parts of Neptunia. Painting—waterproof crayons and other ingenious implements, concreted undersea terra-cotta—had produced works of art that the greatest galleries of the world would not have despised. The live theater and ballet took on a wonder and splendor undreamed of in the upper world of gravity. Ballet—free from the chains of gravity—that Dodge had seen in space. But he had never experienced anything so profoundly stirring as ballet, with the soft buoyant pressure of water to sustain, enhance, add flowing beauty to every movement. It was an experience that left him weak. And yet, apart from isolated highlights, Dodge and Harp mumbled all through this bright vivacious culture, repairing their sub. They were both itching to be away. The busy life of the atoll passed them by.

On the day, Dodge said: "We're on our way back to the farm, Harp. Let's hope we succeed. If we do—there may be the parting of the ways for us."

Accompanied for a short distance by waving mermaids and menfish, the sub drove on south towards their destiny.

CHAPTER FIFTEEN

"You've withheld too many damn secrets from the public already, Henderson," snapped Toxter. His broad-planed shiny face and cigar-clamping jaws assumed their best cartoonist position. Above him on their sponsons the twin jets, fed by the atomic motors, screamed a diminuendo chorus, thrusting the three-decker catamaran directly into the eye of the wind. The sails lay furled along the yards like neat, white sausages fresh from the machine. Sparkling white caps split forth on the waves.

"All right, so there have been things better for the public not to know," Henderson said nervily. His face showed the ravages of a nervous disposition in times of stress. "We announced these people in the Juliana Trench quickly enough."

"Only because you were scared."

Simon Hardy pushed his right hand down over his white hair, smoothing it. He said: "Well, this doesn't get us any farther, gentlemen. Ferenc, here, is no doubt edified by this high-level discussion."

That quietened them. Toxter, Hardy realized with relish, didn't quite have the nerve to ask him to dismiss his aide. A gull shrieked past them, wings stiff. Its beady eye fastened on the barracuda lying limp on the catamaran's upper deck. Captain Pinhorn stood a little to one side, hoping for a lead from Toxter, a little fogged by the swiftness of events. Electronics experts had looked at the

137

electrode, made a few simple remarks, and gone. Now an ichthyologist was dissecting the cuda's brain. That wouldn't take all day. Pinhorn listened whilst the wrangle went on and the cat danced over the waves under the grateful sun.

"So you've actually been able to make men breathe under the sea," said Toxter heavily.

"They've been doing that since the first man stuck a reed in his mouth and went under six inches," said Werner testily and uncharacteristically. Everyone was edgy. The ten-jet bomber had been flown on a trial run and the dummy H-bomb had struck within six hundred yards of the target. The actions to follow in a few days were in everyone's mind. Tempers flared.

"You know what I mean." Toxter took the cigar from his mouth and stabbed with it. "Operating on men, tearing slits under their arms, fouling up their metabolism . . ."

"Oh, stow it, Toxter!" Hardy stalked away across the heaving deck, swung on a heel and said: "The surgical part is child's play, now. U.O.P. has been doing it for years—just as you kept secret your work on cosmic rays. We know." He smiled briefly. "But the Wilkins Corps got hold of it. Unscrupulous surgeons mass-produced menfish —quick, fumbling jobs where the minimum of care was taken. Most of the poor devils can't breathe air any more. It all ties up with the system, I suppose. But the world was starving. Men were clamoring for the pretty baubles in the sky—and their empty bellies had to be filled."

"And so we of Ocean produced the food," Henderson went on deliberately. "So you could send men like Pinhorn here out to the stars. And we succeeded. Now we want to clean up undersea a bit; put some of the results of a too rapid expansion right. So we get a big help from you Space Force people!"

"Well," Toxter rumbled uncomfortably. "We're helping on this Juliana Trench thing."

"Dropping an H-bomb. A fine help."

"Well, what do you suggest we do—go down in a spaceship and shake their hands?"

"Alter that to a deepsea sub—and the answer is yes!"

"It's preposterous! They're dangerous!"

Pinhorn moved to let the ichthyologist up. Over his

shoulder he saw the electronics man coming back at a gallop. Excitement caught the blood in his veins, making them throb.

"Pain center, as we suspected," said the ichthyologist.

"This electrode and battery," panted out the first electronics man, holding the needle out on his palm. "We've never come across anything like it before. It's a minute granule, yet to operate at all it had to develop a potential better than anything we've got of a comparable size."

In the silence the hissing of the jets mounted. A porpoise leaped across the starboard bow and vanished under the port stem. Wind ruffled their hair.

Henderson said: "So the aliens turned our own fish on us. Poetic justice."

The two spiracles jutted from the sand, the valves within slowly opening and closing as the giant ray breathed. Around it, extending for many yards, the coral fans covered low walls and swept upwards in madreporic formations to the seamount's crest. Silver reflections from the surface chased across the bottom in an ever-changing pattern. Tiny fish, red, green, blue, scarlet, darted everywhere. Their colors were no more brilliant than if they had been freshly painted on. Seaweeds trailed, ripe pods hanging from undulating fronds. Eel grass, looking like long reeds, covered irregular patches. A blue crab scuttled, raising a fine white cloud of sand.

As though an invisible gong had been struck, all the fish turned. They poised; and then the sea was empty. Two fast, dark shapes, menacing and full of danger, swept across the ray, not seeing him, rose quickly upwards with lithe, powerful beats of fins. The King of the Sea was on the prowl. The little fish had learned to stay clear of him, here, where there were no nets and corrals, no electric currents to turn them into road-traffic. This was the open range, up near the surface, perched on a narrow ledge of coral around a partially submerged atoll, too small—yet—for human civilization.

One of the dark, terrible shapes made a sound.

"That's as far as we go, Jerry. They never used this section. Too small and too much trouble to work it."

Dodge halted his upward rush, finned more slowly to

float at Harp's side. "So they're not here. No one is here. The whole area stripped, wiped out, gone." He beat a fist into the other hand. "Do you suppose . . ."

"We don't know. The girls weren't alone. There were plenty of other people about—men, I mean, not menfish. Maybe they got them into a balloon. Be safe in there from the cudas."

"I'm hoping you're right."

Harp rolled over onto his back, stared up.

"We'll just have to go back to Neptunia and hope Pop will give us another lead. They've radio there. We'll have to listen to the news broadcasts."

"You crazy? Nothing of all this gets on the air."

"This is too big to be hushed up. If this is internal warfare between Wilkins Corporations—well . . ."

"I hate to admit it; but I think you're right. There's something going on bigger than we know anything about."

Harp was still staring upwards at the silvery-blue dazzle. "Surface is up there. Want to take a look?"

Dodge answered by jackknifing upwards. Harp joined him. They beat upwards with quick, anticipatory fins.

The colors of the fishes about them should have warned them. Even though these fish darted away, quite unlike the more measured retreat of the fish with which they were acquainted, they had seen the brilliance of fin and scale. Of course—they couldn't check the pressure, their internal organs perfectly compensated for that. They rocketed upwards like two surfacing porpoises.

And, like porpoises on one of their supremely abandoned leaps, they soared out of the sea, turned over, and sloshed back. That one quick glimpse had told them nothing. Cautiously, Dodge thrust his head up.

He began to swim. Deliberately, he kept his head above water. Sensations grappled his brain. Light. A searing blaze of light. Fire bludgeoning him, nothing in focus, all distorted. Heat. Dryness. Terrible, burning dryness. Scorching his mouth, parching his throat, crisping his tongue. He gurgled in a watery, horrible gasping as his lungs emptied. Couldn't breathe. Chest hurting. Constriction—he drew his head down into the sea and felt coolness and comfort, liquid salving the abused tender skin, the brittle dryness relaxing. He gulped water into his lungs.

Harp was shaking his head from side to side, and a few shining bubbles drifted from his gills.

"I thought I was dying!"

"Me too."

There was nothing more to say. It was a supreme experience, this return to the world of light and air. They had once more put their heads into their natural habitat—and it had nearly killed them. They sank downwards, finning lightly, lost in thought. Above their heads, two long dark silhouettes, strapped together, passed in a swirling smother of foam from sharp prows.

A light, quick block struck Dodge between the shoulder blades. Automatically, he twisted away, brushing with his hand. The midge-like parasite fish were always on the prowl, darting in to nip at one's gills and raise a fleck of blood. After a time they blended with all the other peculiarities of under ocean. This time the blow came again.

Dodge jackknifed, twisted, stared back.

A little six-inch fish with a bright blue body, gold banded and magnificent, glittering golden fins, fluttered about him, almost falling over itself. Dodge gaped.

"It can't be," he said hollowly. "Sally!" He started to chuckle. "If you aren't Sally, you little devil, then you must be her sister. Well I'm damned."

Sally flicked around and rode his pressure wave as they plunged down. He might have lost the sunshine and air of the upper world and the life before him be all the darker for that; but there was an irrational bubble of elation in him. Sally didn't mean all that, of course. But she was something in this hideous chaos by which he could seek to retain some semblance of sanity, and she was the living proof that when the sea took away it would also return. Dodge, Harp—and Sally—plunged towards their sub.

He knew it was fatuous. He tried despairingly to sink his agony for Elise into a blind, unreasoning acceptance of this catatonic world of water. He tried—and knew he would never succeed.

Beneath him in the depths as he clove headfirst through the water a dark spreading shadow grew. Far larger than their sub, it rose, increasing in size, seeming to his heightened senses the father ray of the beginning of the world, soaring up to engulf its prey.

Shockingly through the watery levels, a shout reached his ears: "Hey! You two! You're wanted!"

The radio said: "All preparations for dropping the bomb have now been finalized. Word from Dahlak Major, UN General Secretary, only is now awaited before the plane takes off on the mission which will rid our planet of the extra-terrestrial menace."

Simon Hardy flicked off the radio and swung towards Dahlak Major, sprawled in a formfit cane chair.

"Well?"

For the fraction of a second a silver-lace mantilla was flung against the sun over the cat's bows. Then the spray, glittering, flew across the decks. The jets had been switched off some time before the ship cut sweetly through the waves under her swelling press of sail. Now—there was no urgency. They had seen what they needed to over the ruined farm beneath the surface. A hot rage burned in them all. Already, two other farms, adjacent on the continental shelf, had been obliterated by stupendous numbers of barracuda.

Over the face of the waters a fleet had assembled, ships of all shapes and tonnages, from heavy-duty deep-sea wreckers to bobbing, brightly shining speed-boats. News of another three farms' destruction had just come through, and the fleet had sped off there like the switching turn and streaming flight of a flock of birds. From the sky a small flying-carpet dropped rapidly towards the catamaran. Hardy looked away from Dahlak Major, scarcely expecting a reply, knowing that UN was even more firmly set on its course of dropping the bomb on the Juliana Trench. He'd had a few bad moments himself, with Henderson and Werner, moments of indecision, when the news of the barracuda onslaught came through. The bomb would sweep up the great trough like a flaming wind, channelled, funnelled, destroying everything on the seafloor. His mind shied away from that; he looked tiredly at the descending flying-carpet.

It hovered a few feet above the rolling deck and a man descended a nylon ladder, his thin arms and legs working as though unaccustomed to gravity. When he reached the deck and turned to face Hardy, the old sea-veteran let out a roar of surprised greeting.

"Eli! You old bad-penny!" He ran forward, right hand outstretched. "No reports from you, son, thought you'd bought it along with the rest."

Eli clicked his plastic set of teeth, smiling. He was lean and starved looking, yet his salute was crisp.

"Reporting back, Admiral. Plenty of evidence on the press-ganging—and some on the hi-jacking." Over drinks he elaborated on what had happened to him on his assignment to be taken up as a slave, then to escape and report back to U.O.P. The trickiest part, he said, was in concealing his status as a manfish and using breathing equipment. He heard about the other agents who had not returned. He tightened his lips when told of the man who had returned—dying—from the Artful Dodger's farm. He was interrupted towards the end by Captain Pinhorn, who had strolled up with Pierre Ferenc to see what the excitement was about.

Pinhorn said: "Hold it. You say two men and two girls escaped from a balloon you were hidden in when a U.O.P. patrol made a raid. You shot a guard to facilitate their escape . . ."

"Kept a little needle gun under my singlet—wore that all the time on account of I was an old man. Old! Hah!" He didn't spit, but it would have fitted. "Yeah. Short, square guy, tough, used a harpoon like he'd been born with one in his mouth." Pinhorn shook his head. Eli went on: "The other one was a real he-man type hero . . ." he described him. And the girls. He wasn't old, wasn't Eli.

"That was Commander Dodge," Pinhorn said emphatically.

Into the babble of speculation following that a second flying carpet hovered and a second man—big, fat, domineering—descended to the heaving decks.

It was evident that Dahlak Major and Toxter wanted to ask questions; but they all pivoted to regard Mr. Grosvenor walk towards them, his gross bulk giving the impression that he waddled. His face was engorged and he breathed with a dry rasping.

Henderson bristled like a dog scenting a stranger.

"Glad you could come, Mr. Grosvenor," he said stiffly.

"I've spent a heck of a long while down on Trident," began Grosvenor. "And now you haul me back from my farm at this juncture. Whatever it is you want to see me about must be very important if it's more urgent than the mess down there."

"We have some questions," Henderson began smoothly. "Dahlak Major, as UN secretary, would like further information about the depredations before ordering the bomb . . ."

"Why wait!" Grosvenor coughed and touched a bloody handkerchief to his lips. "Drop the bomb, the biggest one you've got, on those murdering monsters."

"There speaks the world," murmured Hardy.

The sun shone warmly. The waves made pleasant guitar sounds. A few gulls rode the wind with arched wings. It was strange to think of the terror and death and merciless ferocity prisoned beneath their keels down there in the blue silence of the depths. It was more than just the difference between two worlds; it was the difference between two entire conceptions of dream worlds.

"—fish for inhuman experiments," Dahlak Major was saying. "I don't think the council will view that with favor, Mr. Grosvenor."

"I see." Mr. Grosvenor dabbed his mouth with a bloody handkerchief. "I'm here on trial, am I? Well, the U.O.P. do it, don't they? They have fish to hunt down innocent men on the farms! Ask them about sticking needles in fishes' brains!"

"Sure we do, Grosvenor," said Hardy, controlling himself savagely and oddly disturbed by the sight of the bedabbled handkerchief. "But we operate on the pleasure principle, not the pain, as you do."

"Why not use dolphins and porpoises?" said Toxter vaguely. "I've always heard they are friendly to man."

Hardy laughed unpleasantly. "People have a friendly feeling towards them, you mean. It's a stimulating experience to see them all plunging and gleaming at the forefoot of a ship. It's because they're mammals; there is a feeling of affinity. Experiments have been tried to control them like we do dogs; there's even been some success. But the techniques of broadcasting directly to electrode-controlled brain areas leaped ahead so much, that clumsy methods like that were soon outdated. Anyway, we need watchdogs that can stay on duty beneath the surface all the time, and don't have to take time out to surface for some fresh air."

"The U.O.P. are nothing but a bunch of . . ." Grosvenor started to say; but Hardy cut him off with a quick jerk of his stump. There was a rage in him against the unwanted pity clouding his judgment. He spoke quite savagely.

"Your surgery is terrible! Even you can't breathe air properly—look at you, suffering as though you were a fish! And we have reason to believe that you've been performing even worse jobs on your slaves. Yes—slaves!"

"I don't understand," said Grosvenor puffily. He threw the handkerchief over the side and reached for a fresh one. "Slaves? What slaves? If you mean our indentured workers . . . ?"

"Look, man, if you can't stand it—go and put your head in a bucket of water. We can talk from there."

Grosvenor hesitated, his little eyes mean and calculating. Then he coughed again, staining his handkerchief, and that decided him. A sailor drew a bucket of water and Grosvenor thankfully thrust his head in and drew deep breaths of water. The others could feel his relief almost physically. A hose was left pumping a slow supply of water into the bucket; water ran from Grosvenor's gill slits and stained his shirt and coat, and formed a trickling stream across the deck.

He said, the sound hollow and booming: "God, I was on fire!"

Ferenc said aside to Pinhorn: "Trouble is the mucus-secreting cells of the lungs; these blundering slave-surgeons have to remove it to allow sea-water to pass, extra viscous, you see. But they don't bother to provide fresh replacements for when you breathe air—so the lungs harden. Grosvenor's only had half the job done on him. Hasn't even got an operculum."

"But his operation is better than those slaves of his,

right?" whispered Pinhorn. He stared at Grosvenor as though physically repelled.

"Now then, Grosvenor," said Hardy. "I know all about your slaves. And it's no good calling them indentured workers. When UN outlawed the economic man-trap system where a man was cajoled into the sea and then found everything so expensive that he could never buy himself out, or his passage home—a sweet racket that was! You were in such deep waters—hah!—that you and your like went ahead and took unwilling workers, forced them to work, press-ganged them into menfish. You became so rich and powerful you could afford to set up your own little empires out there on the shelves. You took men, pressed them to work, denied them a right to return. If that isn't slavery, what is?"

A series of gurgles came from the bucket. Grosvenor hadn't expected such a direct attack, and Hardy ploughed on, condemning, branding, castigating.

Pinhorn, his dark featured faced set, stood grimly looking on, seeing nothing ludicrous in the spectacle of a portly man carrying on a conversation with his head in a bucket of water. He was anxious to find out more about this undersea world; but Eli had just brought in the first clue to the whereabouts of Jerry Dodge. At last he had something to work on, however slender the thread might be.

Ferenc slipped away from his side across the sun-drenched deck in response to a call from a radioman. When he returned from the bridge his face was eager. He said quickly to Pinhorn: "Things are shaping up, Pin!" And then, cutting across the conversation, to Hardy: "Excuse me, sir. Message just in from patrol eleven."

"Well?"

"They've picked up a sub-tow balloon about fifty miles south of here. Towing it to Trident. Full of slaves and workers and guards—the usual thing Eli was talking about. All from the Artful Dodger's farm, escaped when the barracuda attacked." He paused.

Hardy, slowly, said: "Very interesting, Pierre. And?"

Ferenc's faith in his chief was upheld. The old boy knew when there was more news. Ferenc said impressively: "A girl aboard called Miss Elise Tarrant. She and two

Siamese friends wish to lay charges against Mr. Grosvenor for kidnapping, press-ganging, pressure to work—oh, all kinds of meaty charges."

He beamed. "They want to throw the book."

CHAPTER SIXTEEN

Everybody was talking at once. Hardy, jubilantly: "At last! We've got him!" Pinhorn: "Where's Dodge?" Dahlak Major: "Most irregular." Henderson: "So it's broken at last, thank God!" Pinhorn: "Where's Dodge?" Werner: "We'll brief the best counsel . . ." Pinhorn: "Where's Dodge?" Grosvenor threw his head from the bucket with a scattering of shining drops, a wild look of fear touching his blunt features with the dawning realization that his world was sinking. "How did she get there?" he demanded plaintively. Pinhorn: "Where's Commander Dodge?"

Pinhorn went on saying that, over and over, until everyone else stopped and looked at him. He took a deep breath. "Where is Commander Dodge, please, Pierre?"

Ferenc shook his head. "No news, Pin. I asked. Miss Tarrant saw him once after their escape when Eli helped them—she didn't know that, of course. Just before the barracuda attacked." He paused and looked over Pinhorn's shoulders at the knife-blade horizon, then uncomfortably stared straight at Pinhorn. "He was a manfish."

"Oh, no!" Pinhorn was aghast. It was more than conventional horror; he had an above the average empathy with spacemen; he guessed, and cringed from, what Dodge had been through. All he had heard about the butchering methods of the farms welled up in his mind. "You mean —he can't breathe air?" He did not wait for an answer. He knew it. "On the Arthur Dodge farm, his own farm, inherited from his uncle and fouled up by you, Grosvenor, you fat slug."

Pinhorn stepped forward and put his right fist in Grosvenor's mouth, jetting water from the gill slits, and then kicked the manfish in the stomach. Grosvenor went down, unconscious, sprawled across the bucket. Ferenc righted it, leaned over and shoved the limp head in and played the hose on it. No one said anything.

Then Eli said reflectively: "I think you're kinda doing the fat boy an injustice, son." He clicked his teeth. "I wasn't in the Artful Dodger's little mob when your pals escaped. It wasn't Grosvenor who press-ganged them in the first place. They musta been caught by him in a hi-jacking deal after they left that sub-tow balloon."

"That sounds improbable. Miss Tarrant would know that, anyway. Yet she is pressing charges . . ."

Ferenc said: "I know Danny Agostini. Grosvenor's head chopper. He's hopped enough to do anything. Miss Tarrant said definitely that he had caught them in his sub . . ."

"What a situation," Hardy said, and whistled. "Young Dodge, hi-jacked by his own employees and turned into a manfish by them. Well—we'd never have looked there for him. We'd have assumed that the red-carpet was laid down."

Pinhorn said it for them all: "Where is he now?"

Dahlak Major rose from his cane formfit. His careful face expressed concern. He said: "This is all most disturbing and I do appreciate your concern over the welfare of the Space Force Officer. But it is all most irregular. There have now been six Bishop Wilkins Corporations destroyed by deliberately maddened barracuda, controlled and inflamed by the aliens trespassing in our waters. And I am about to give the order for the H-bomb to be dropped." He clucked his tongue. "I sincerely hope that Commander Dodge is not near the Juliana Trench at the present time."

Silence. Then Hardy, knowing it was useless, again attempted to delay the dropping of the bomb. He was waving his arm about when a rating put his head out of the control cabin in the rear of the bridge and shouted: "Got a strange ping here, sir."

Hardy went forward. Henderson followed him and Minister of Aquiculture Werner took over the job of wearing down Dahlak Major. They hadn't been very successful so far.

In the cabin Henderson said: "Where are we?"

Hardy, looking out the window at the rolling sea, grunted, and checked back on the echo sounds. He stared at the bottom contours and then said: "Over the Easternmost end of the Artful Dodger's range. Don't think they use it much. Grosvenor would know. If poor Dodge is finished—and those barracuda leave little hope—then I don't know who the farm belongs to. Where's this echo?"

The asdic showed a large ping on the screen. It was rising upwards rapidly from the depths. No one recognized it. Two smaller pings were shown, quite near the surface.

Outside on the deck Pinhorn was viciously gripping the rail. He stared with unseeing eyes across the sun-dazzled billows. Ferenc, beside him, could find nothing to say. He looked across the troubled surface, thinking of the cool blue depths, when he saw two fish burst from the water and flop over and go sliding back.

"Porpoises, how charming," said someone at his back.

Ferenc saw that sharp picture in his mind, the quick bright flash of pink, the shape—he shouted suddenly.

"They weren't porpoises!" And then he ripped his plastic flippers from their strap around his neck where U.O.P. personnel carried equipment when out of water, slid his feet in and took a short, splay-footed run to the rail and went over in a clean cutting dive.

Dancing with impatience, fired by a feeling that something important was happening, Pinhorn struggled into a face-mask with attached spun-glass cylinders, one of the short-period masks, no time for the big ones now, and flip-flopped down the ladder and splashed into the water after Ferenc. Hardy ran from the cabin. Henderson followed. Dahlak Major, Toxter and Werner ran to the rail and stared into the concealing water. Tension screwed everyone's nerves.

Just two porpoises? Or two dead men? Or what?

As that human shout penetrated the empty wastes of water, Dodge checked his plunge. Sally pirouetted, sweeping round in a tight circle to finish up again on his dying pressure wave. Dodge floated, finning lightly. Harp went on, then jackknifed and swept back. They all stared up.

A gleaming figure plummeted down to them, sheathed in clinging air-bubbles and trailing a glistening line of bubbles like the silver-blurred stroke of a sword. There was the impression of immensely powerful fins, the almost physical impact of water being sliced through as though it were melted grease under a branding iron. Harp and Dodge slung their harpoons forward, tensing, ready for anything.

The shape resolved into a manfish. There was something about him that was strange to Dodge's eyes; but in the immediate impact of wonder, the dissimilarity between himself and this stranger eluded him. He looked tremendously powerful and completely at home beneath the waves.

Again the shout, a short, flung shock-wave of sound that drove far farther underwater than any previous shouts Dodge had heard. He knew his own range was negligible by comparison. "Hey! Want to talk to you two!"

The stranger flew up to them, halted in a quick, casually easy flick of fins and hung, staring at them. Dodge saw the broad shoulders, the easy rhythm of this manfish, and felt strangely humble, knew with deep conviction that here was a true manfish, in comparison with whom he was only a tiddler.

"Who are you? Don't you know what's been going on?"

Dodge knew the answer to that too damn well, he knew what had been going on, all right. But he certainly wasn't going to tell this newcomer, who was quite possibly one of the devils controlling the barracuda. Almost, he triggered his harpoon. Still—he might know about Elise . . .

At Dodge's side, Harp tensed then pressed closer. Dodge started to say: "What's your business?" when Harp let out a whoop that rolled away undersea like a watery banshee.

"Pierre! By all that's holy—Pierre!"

"Who the—Harp! By the tentacles of daddy octopus himself—Harp!" The two menfish gripped hands, stunned by the encounter. "I thought you were teaching maiden

151

ladies how to embrace the strong male sea with breathing equipment?"

"So I was. Until they decided I'd be better off working on the farm."

"Manfish. How come?"

"They thought I'd work better that way. It's a long story . . ."

"You—you were the square guy that Eli . . ." Ferenc was squeaking it all out, unable to put his words into proper order. "Then this is—this is the spaceman—Pinhorn—you must be Commander Jeremy Dodge!"

Three extraordinarily puzzled menfish stared at one another. Below them, as introductions were made, rising like boiling milk in a saucepan a spreading shadow exploded outwards with the rapidity of its ascent. Aboard the catamaran above, that huge shape creating an outsize ping on the asdic screen had now claimed all attention after Pinhorn had disappeared over the side. Captain Pinhorn, Space Force, flew down into the depths of Earth's blue sea and there made contact with Commander Jeremy Dodge, Space Force. It was a meeting more macabre than any meeting of those two on the explored planets and satellites of the solar system could ever have been.

"Jerry, you old space-hog. Found you at last!"

"Pin. What, the Space Force in trouble again?"

Above them the surface was like a cloud-riven silver sky over some alien unworldly planet.

"You better come back with us, Jerry, right away. Admiral Hardy would like to hear what you have to say." Ferenc smiled. "We're going to build up such a case against Grosvenor that he'll never squirm out of it."

"Grosvenor?" said Dodge sharply. "He was the guy I was supposed to be meeting when Elise and I . . ." He stopped talking. Then, his words quite distinct in the clogging water: "Sorry, fellows. Can't go topside, for two reasons. Can't breathe air. Must find Miss Tarrant."

"But Miss Tarrant is being taken to Trident," Ferenc was saying excitedly as Pinhorn tried to flap himself round to stay with the others. But his breathing gear and lack of fins made him an easy prey to the rising bubble of water being forced through the surrounding sea. He went racing away above, unable, as were the others, to fin hard and stay with the rising wash of water being driven from the swollen black shape below.

Pinhorn was swept away. "Leave him," Ferenc shouted. "He'll be picked up. Below . . ."

"Killer whale?" asked Harp. They were all tensed; but no one seemed frightened—yet.

"No," said Ferenc decisively. "Too big. I've seen them. Seen them muzzle up to a damned fat Gray Whale, force the poor thing's mouth open and stick their heads in and start feeding on the beast's tongue. Very tasty morsel, that."

"What is it?" yelled Dodge.

Beneath them, now, the sea had turned from blue to black. The shape fanned out under them like the father ray of time; there was even a short tail, too. Riding the criss-crossing currents forced through the water, Sally clung to Dodge as he stayed with the others; they were like midges dancing in a thermal updraft over a huge beast's back in the tropical sun. But, inevitably, they couldn't stay there. As the water broke in confusion around them, roaring and buffeting them and sluiced down over sleek flanks, they were sundered apart, spilled away in an undersea avalanche. Dodge saw his companions threshing water, saw them plucked from him as he, in turn, was sucked down and away on the other side.

He went over and over in the water, rolling around and down the monstrous body.

And as he went, thrust by tons of water through more water, he saw in the body creating such undersea turbulence, rows of portholes, neat mechanically perfect fins and rearward-pointing venturis.

He refused to believe it was a spaceship.

Not because it was like no spaceship he had ever seen— he, like all spacemen, was perpetually ready for the day when "They" contacted us from outside the system—no; the reason he knew it was no spaceship was something he might not have bothered about prior to his underwater career. Any spaceship designed to withstand one atmosphere within will be precious little use when subjected to ten atmospheres' external pressure. It could only be a submarine. But Dodge did not like the remembered words of Pierre Ferenc when they'd been so arbitrarily swept apart.

"What is it?" Dodge had said. And Pierre had replied somberly: "I'm very much afraid I know what it is. And I don't like what I know." And then the monster had interposed its thrusting bulk between them, and now Dodge was sorting himself out beneath the swelling flanks, with Sally gyrating as a golden mote in the corner of his eye, and wondering if this was the end of the world.

Once before there had been the opportunity of escape leaving friends to their fate. This time, although still possessed of the conviction that Pierre was as tough underwater as anyone Dodge had ever met there, he again could not make himself fly off and leave them. Into the bargain, exciting, enigmatic, was the question of the submarine; fly off and leave that with its mystery all unexplored? Not likely!

An oval of yellow light sprang into being on the metal flank. Dodge expected anything. Mermen—in the traditional sense with tails and flukes, not the familiar menfish; a swarm of crazed barracuda; alien beings from another star; a grim posse of the Under Ocean Patrol; even Captain Kitser come to take into custody his errant soldier.

He was totally unprepared for the voice which said: "Attention. We wish to be friends. Repeating. We wish to be friends. Please do not be afraid. Repeating. Please do not be afraid."

The insane thought hit Dodge: *"Suppose I didn't speak English?"*

He tried to say something; and his brain iced up.

He deliberately threw his mind back to Space Force procedure in the little blue manual you were passed out on oral examination: "Procedures to be Adopted on Encountering Extra-Terrestrial Intelligence."

But—the possibility had never been foreseen that an officer of the Space Force would first contact alien intelligences under the seas of his parent Earth.

The situation just wasn't in the book.

It was giant cart-before-the-horse arrangement.

Dodge shouted: "Yes. We want to be friends, too. Who

are you? Where are you from?" And then remembered. Questions and answers on a one-for-one basis. Treat as equals—equals, hell! That damn great sub could knock him out of the water like a squashed sea-urchin.

A dark silhouette appeared in the yellow oval of radiance flooding from the hatch.

"There has been a grave mistake." The voice boomed out, magnified, carrying clearly, not quite correctly accented. Dodge wondered if Harp and his pal Pierre could hear it, wherever they were now on the other side of the sub. "Are you a person in authority? If not, can you contact someone in authority? Repeating. Can you contact someone in authority?"

"With all this repeating lark, you get the impression they're not sure we can hear them." The voice was Harp's, coming from the blankness of the shadow beneath the sub. Dodge knew that in that shadow he would be able to see clearly, all the microscopic flecks in the water robbed of the scintillating illumination which made them visible as a fog in the water. He watched as Harp and Ferenc flew out of that region of darkness.

"Yes. I am a person of authority," he shouted as loudly as he could, trying to control his amplifier to give a clear bell like sound. "And we can contact others of the government of Earth. How well do you speak English?"

"Well enough, as you must appreciate." The shape outlined in the yellow hatch had not moved. What might be a head tilted; Dodge knew it was peering down at the two new arrivals.

"My friends," Dodge said quickly. He felt unsure, emotionally, abysmally unsure. What should he do at this critical juncture in the history of the Earth? A wrong word, a mistaken meaning, the slightest slip could mean a protracted period of turmoil and confusion, possibly even war. Interstellar war might be, thankfully, an impossibility; but if these aliens—and how he knew they were aliens!—were so well at home in Earth's seas as they obviously were, the fight would all take place here, in Earth's own oceans.

And that must not be allowed to happen.

The alien said: "Your government intend to drop a thermonuclear bomb onto our city. We would discuss the situation with them before action is taken. We can explain everything. Repeating. We can explain everything."

Dodge wasn't quite sure he knew what the alien was talking about. Into that thought came Ferenc's strong voice.

"We know you interfered with Earthly fish of a particularly vicious character; we know you set the barracuda on our peaceful farms. Is that an act of friendship?"

Dodge didn't know whether to shout at Ferenc to shut up and to let the spaceman do the talking, or to allow horror and revulsion at the aliens' crime overcome him. Certainly, if this were true, it made nonsense of the aliens' claims to friendship. He began to flipper quietly away.

"Hold it, Dodge!" That was Ferenc.

He flew rapidly towards the oval light. "I am Commander Pierre Ferenc of Earth's Under Ocean Patrol. I can asure you of a hearing with the government and with the chiefs of Under Ocean." Harp flew stolidly at his shoulder, silent, watchful, hands lightly grasping his harpoon.

Dodge was torn between emotion and what he conceived of as his duty. "They set the barracuda on us!" he yelled. The words were out before he realized he had spoken. He was thinking of Elise. He had a claustrophobic memory of diving into that sub with half his flipper chewn off by the hideous jaws of a cuda, of the stifling fear there in that darkness. Of the dead engineer. Of the ripped-up sharks, the dead menfish—perhaps one had been Knut. Even Captain Kitser and his "All right!" attained a measure of worth in his mind. No man should have to die under the maddened fangs of insane barracuda. He changed direction, flew in towards the two menfish and the alien in the hatch, not quite sure what he intended to do. The alien still had not moved. It was a ticklish moment.

This Ferenc was a fast thinker. He said quickly, softly: "I told you, Dodge. Miss Tarrant is safe."

"Yeah." The information hadn't penetrated before. Dodge marvelled. He'd been developing a one track mind.

"What is the trouble?" That was the alien. There was nothing in the voice that might be construed as emotion; an alien contriving to speak an unfamiliar language through the stifling medium of water, it would have been a miracle if there had been recognizable overtones in the voice. Dodge flew up to Ferenc, floated.

Carefully, Dodge said: "There is no trouble."

He was still unsure just how much initiative he should allow Ferenc, for all that the manfish was a U.O.P. officer, and therefore likely to be completely familiar with undersea matters. This was Space Force business. He moved in closer. Show no fear, said the book. Be politely aggressive. From nowhere came the cynical wonder whether any "Procedures for Dealing with Alien Cultures" had ever been scheduled for the Under Ocean forces. It was most unlikely.

And with that thought, too, came the sickening realization that so far all the initiative had been with the alien standing—if it was standing—in the hatch. The Earthmen had been behaving as though they were dumb idiots, puzzled, divided in their councils; behaving like a typical cross-section of Earthpeople in fact. And those barracuda ...

"Why did you turn those killer fish loose on helpless farms? There were many deaths of Earth people. Much damage was done. How can we trust you?"

"It was a mistake. You have to trust us. Repeating. You have to trust us." Was there a hint of desperation in the voice? Or was it wishful thinking?

"Why?"

Before any answer to that could be given, Dodge saw Harp and Ferenc drop alarmingly, as though they were in a bottomless elevator shaft. They retained their postures in the water; but went straight down. They dwindled as though diminishing powder had been dropped on them from the pages of some necromancer's book, and Dodge whirled to stare at the alien, a fear he would not acknowledge brushing his mind. The alien had not moved.

A cry came from the plummeting men. Ferenc.

"Away, fast, Harp!" The two menfish struck out powerfully with hands and flippers. "Fresh water! Danger!"

Dodge knew, then. A stream of fresh water flowing up from some fissure in the seamount away in the blueness, a common phenomena of the ocean floor, this time, as always, had brought lurking menace to the menfish. Buoyancy was immediately affected. But, most serious, fresh water is injurious to the lungs. And it had to happen now; just as they were attempting to negotiate with aliens —the aliens would believe they had to deal with a weak and puny race.

Well—wasn't that true?

Ferenc and Harp, breathing and blowing salt water gustily, flew up to rejoin him. The alien now chose to make his answer to Dodge's blunt query.

His body rose; he was balancing daintily upon two large and powerful flippers. The body was a glistening black, caught in some hidden orange reflection from the lock at his rear, so that molten fire seemed to outline him, gleaming in dramatic relief. A single hand came up—a hand like a human hand.

"You must trust us as we trust you. We have read your radio messages and the signals transmitted by your primitive ultra-sonic equipment. Your decision to destroy us with a thermonuclear weapon filled us with horror. We have lived long and peacefully in your oceans, we have never harmed you . . ."

Dodge and Ferenc spoke as one, yet their queries were different. Dodge said: "What about the barracuda?"

"I repeat our apologies. It was a mistake and we can explain."

Ferenc had said: "What about that sub you dragged down?"

Dodge, trying to repress his natural instincts of anger and resentment, scarcely heard Ferenc's question and the answer it elicited. Mistake! The explanations would have to be good—exceedingly good. Then he became interested in the conversation.

The alien in answer to Ferenc's question said: "We were intrigued. We felt that you were visiting us. We drew your vessel toward our city and—and it crumpled up. We were deeply shocked. We did not fully understand at that time. Do you understand?"

Ferenc flippered in to float quietly beside Dodge.

"I think so." The U.O.P. man was quite obviously trying to forget something. "We live at the surface of the seas. You live in the depths. So it was natural that you should not realize that our sub would be crushed by the pressure." He lifted his head. "I lost friends on those vessels. Good friends."

"You have our fullest sympathy." The voice was completely emotionless, metallic, artificially reproduced. And yet Dodge, for one, believed what it said.

Ferenc said, in a quick aside to Dodge: "The crews of the crushed subs weren't menfish. I'm undecided whether to let on that we aren't exactly representative of our race."

"Let things take their own course." Dodge rolled his harpoon round onto his shoulders out of the way. "Let things take their own sweet way." He managed not to add that he had received training to cope with this situation. He had a nasty suspicion that all the training in the world —or off or under it—was negligible compared with two seconds conversation with a real live alien.

The alien had lifted himself another six inches and now orange light haloed his head, showing in bold relief the bulging, human-type cranium.

"We know your government is divided on the use of the thermonuclear bomb. We know that a"—the alien paused, then went on with assurance—"an Admiral Simon Hardy is opposed to its use. We obtained a bearing on his transmission source and rose to attempt to make contact. We, too, are divided in our counsels. The parties who launched the attack of the fish upon your farms have been finally eclipsed and have been placed in protective custody. For myself and my friends, we wish to apologize deeply, most sincerely, for the damage and we will make what reparations we can."

Dodge didn't say: "Pshaw!" But he felt like it. This whole situation didn't smell right. There was a phoney ring to it—or was he still out of focus in his thinking since his experiences beneath the sea? He knew that he had changed, both physically and in his thinking—as who wouldn't?—but he could not say that he had developed. Certainly, he didn't seem to have the same black-and-white summation that he had had before; he found—to his perplexed annoyance—that he wanted to believe what the alien said. He was tired of fighting and struggling, and the continuous anxiety of personal safety—and the tearing fears for Elise. He wanted an armchair and a comfortable pair of slippers.

Feeling like that, floating silently in the deep-blue depths with the curved flanks of the submarine dwindling into the haze, he heard Ferenc in busy communion with an ultrasound set on his chest. Ferenc nodded vehemently once or twice as he spoke, driving home a point. Eventually he looked up at the alien. He moved his flippers automatically to keep station on the hatch.

"I have been in communication with Admiral Hardy. He is most anxious to meet you. We have managed to delay the bomb dropping by one hour. No longer—they do not wish to delay it beyond the fuel-capacity of the bomber to return safely to its base, and they're not certain enough yet to withdraw it. So you'll have to convince us inside" —he glanced at his waterproof watch—"five hours. Maximum. Can do?"

The alien's body dropped onto the hatch flooring. His voice, still as strong through the amplifier, had a gasping sound to it. "Yes. We understand. Thank you."

Dodge, looking and listening and wondering, saw that the alien's strangely human head was human only in the cranial structure; the body was like a porpoise's, with the snout much foreshortened and that sapien sweep of forehead above, oddly disconcerting, was the only truly human feature—apart from the hands—of the alien's physiology. But then, brain and hands, weren't they the hallmarks of intelligence? And in the sea an upright posture was unnecessary, was a positive hindrance.

The three Earthmen moved in closer. The alien's arms were not human arms; but, quite apart from the hands, they were true arms in every sense, very far removed from the fumbling lobe-fins of the crossopterygians. On one wrist Dodge caught the dull gleam of a wristlet. Twin huge eyes regarded them—then, in the instant that Dodge saw that those eyes were not eyes at all, but goggles faced with dark glass. He saw also that the skin was not skin, but some black material forming a pressure suit—a suit that bulged shiningly from internal forces.

Of course—the alien was dressed in his equivalent of a space suit; he'd need it, too, up here where the pressure was a mere hundred pounds to the square inch. Down there in the abyss, where the pressure cracked on tons per square inch, would be at home. The swift rise of the alien craft showed that it was pressurized—the aliens would otherwise have bloated like those deep-sea fish cruelly and quickly dragged from the depths in nets. The alien moved lumpily back. He gestured.

"I have been in communication also," he said. "My leader in our city would talk with an Earthman, try to convince you that we mean you no harm."

"That's all right," Ferenc said. "We'd be happy to talk to him. My chief can hold off five hours, after that, if your story doesn't hold together . . ."

"We have no time to lose, then." The alien shuffled backwards and distinctly over the amplifier came the muffled laboring gasps of his breathing. He again gestured. Dodge saw, with only a mild shock, that he was indicating that they should step on the hatch coaming.

Dodge realized suddenly that the Earthmen had been behaving like a group of boys warily watching a wounded snake, aware that it could not harm them unless they approached it. Without being fully aware of all his motives, he flicked his fins and dived forward to sail up, and drop neatly onto the hatch flooring. The alien was no more than three feet away.

Before Dodge could say anything, the alien spoke.

"Good. I am glad you decided to trust us."

The alien was still speaking, but Dodge's thoughts raced chaotically; the stilted phraseology that very naturally infused this being's speech had induced a corresponding stiffness in his own and in Ferenc's. Something of the aura of the situation must have influenced them all; the dimly perceived and reluctantly accepted dictation of the propriety of outside events that forced their hands, willy-nilly. This was indeed a moment of supreme importance not only to the people of Earth, but also to the people living far below in the seas. Nothing flippant, it might be thought, could possibly intrude. They were behaving like civilized members of society, not quite correctly introduced, who wished to create a good impression upon each other, and yet at the same time, ironically conscious of the undercurrent of raw laughter bubbling from the onlookers.

161

The alien was saying: "Now we must act quickly if we are to see our leader in the city and then return here before five of your hours are up."

All Dodge could think of to say was: "Down there?"

CHAPTER SEVENTEEN

If, when Dodge had first penetrated into the undersea mystery of the planet, he had thought he was entering a new world, then the experience of diving twenty-five thousand feet showed him two fresh and quite distinct worlds. They lay under the two worlds of Earth with which he was familiar, forming the lower slices of a planetary sandwich. He wouldn't have cared to say which of the four affected him most.

The alien's water-lock took in the three Terrans and, gradually and with much foreboding, the pressure was built up. Apart from a singing in the ears—distinct from that other singing, which Dodge now realized for the first time had ceased, since it began back on the farm—the symptoms of a deep dive were simply not noticeable. Harp had said, uneasily: "The blood gets too viscid under pressure. Heart can't pump it."

Ferenc, with forced cheerfulness, pooh-poohed that idea. "Blood's very like sea-water," he said confidently. "Almost impossible to compress—only a negligible fraction at mermaids twenty-five. Your heart'll be all right, Harp."

And so it was.

Standing now inside the alien sub, sinking down through the oppressive blackness of the ocean the three Earthmen stared out at sights reserved exclusively for deep divers and nightmares. Lights. Lights everywhere. The utter blackness vanished and re-appeared like distorting scenery in a

163

masque—now it covered the eyes like mourners' crepe;
now it peeled away as phosphorescent lights exploded all
around. Shrimps blew up, giving off clouds of pinkish light,
seeking to hide themselves from the jaws of darting agile
fish. Barbels and tendrils trailed, electric tripwires for un-
wary fish. Small grotesque fish blazing like ocean liners with
rows of portholes, and red and green navigation lights
passed and repassed the port. One fish Dodge saw with a
fascinated revulsion, was all skinless lower jaw. It hurled
itself forward, jolted by a huge naked muscle, trapped
a squirming fish larger than the hunter—then the jaw
almost with powers of independent motion hinged out
and back, so that it seemed to have acted like a bucket-
grab, scooping up its prey. It took some time for Dodge
to get over that.

Far above their heads the long rollers marched end-
lessly towards the east; the sun shining from their foam
flecked flanks, spindrift hurtling merrily on the breeze.

Down in the depths all was quietness and stealth.

Until they passed the giant squids. Dodge caught the
briefest glimpse of a sounding whale struggling with a
squid, then the sub was plunging on, down into blackness
like a vertigo, sliding through the still water, a giant
shadow in darkness.

It was like seeing a city in haloed illumination battling
creeping arms of fog. Lights glowed everywhere, surprising
him. On rounded domes, on tall spires, on pinnacles of
rock that towered and leaned without fear of gravity over
vast silent areas nested with neat round igloo dwellings,
the luster glowed like witch-fire. Dodge, looking from the
port, tried to conjure up what it was that the city reminded
him of—and knew in all his experiences on the alien
worlds of space he had never encountered anything so
eerie, so haunting, as this city drowned beneath the oceans
of Earth.

They were conducted through a wide central plaza and
Dodge found a strange familiarity with the concept of
building in three dimension without need for flyovers and
escalators and the dry-neck paraphernalia of ascending
and descending vertically. All about them the porpoise-
like inhabitants flew and gambolled and formed an undulating line, a procession that swept them onto the central

block of subdued brilliance where dwelt the alien they had come to see. He was old. Personally old. His skin grayed in puckered patches quite unlike the healthy blue-black sheen of the aliens' skins. His eyes, huge, weak, fathomless, regarding them with a depth of feeling that Dodge found disconcerting. The alien who had brought them said: "This is the Prime Minister. That is the nearest term I can find in your language to explain his position and function."

There was nothing odd, now, in meeting and talking to an alien beneath your own seas. This alien had that radiating aura of confidence that comes only to those who are born of nobility, who have achieved near-divine status in their own lifetimes—or who are dying. Dodge thought that perhaps this alien possessed all those three attributes.

The conversation was short. The extraterrestrials had no desire for war; they wished merely to live and let live. The party who had performed the operations on the barracuda had been condemned, the action, even in face of the expected assault of a hydrogen bomb, outraging all public opinion. They had been deposed and were all now on their way back to their parent planet, there to stand trial. As the Prime Minister said: "We are not an old race; not as old as yours, Earthman. We dwell beneath the seas of a planet light years away and the concept of space and stars was something beyond our comprehension. How would anyone living on the surface with this great mass of water and darkness pressing upon him know of the other star-filled reaches? To us, you live tenuously supported high above the surface on the rocky peaks of mountain ranges. What you find to breathe up there was the source of many academic discussions until we learned your language. But I digress. We met and were befriended by a race who had conquered space. They gave us spaceships, taught us celestial navigation, opened our eyes to wonders we had never believed possible. Because ours is a young race we are spreading, seeking new lands, forever restless and roaming."

There was silence, the thick words falling into pools of shadowy vacuum. Dodge contrasted the virility of a young race with this old alien's personal future. He found a great pity in him. Geriatrics ought, perhaps, to receive far more conscious effort of discovery . . .

The alien was speaking again. "We would live in your oceans, here on the floor. We cannot live on the mountain peaks, we do not wish to do so. I am aware that you have two different levels of civilization; one on the lower borders of the upper shelves, where my people might possibly be able to live continually gasping for oxygen. Above that line—there is nothing for us."

Ferenc said: "We cannot agree to anything. We can only take your proposals back. But I can tell you that my government will not concede the continental shelves. They produce food—we must work them. We would have to fight first."

The alien moved a weak hand. "I know. We do not want them. I have seen something of your system there, the brutality, the slavery, the surgery performed on fishes. Yet you have no hesitation in blaming our wayward sons for their surgery in response to a threat."

Alarmed, Dodge said quickly: "I do not anticipate great opposition to the plan. There are forces which demand all of the seas, even these lightless deeps"—he gestured round a little helplessly as though to assure the alien—"though there is nothing here for us that we cannot find more easily elsewhere. We cannot give you guarantees. But we can assure you of our whole-hearted support." He was thinking of the spaceships that could cross the interstellar void—and of the aliens who had given those ships away. This meeting would have far-reaching repercussions away from the seas of Earth, out there in the frosty glare of space. Space . . .

He dragged his attention back and caught Ferenc saying something about the urgency of returning, five hours, decompression . . . The three Terrans, their minds filled, whirling, awed and yet uplifted, moved to return to the submarine, which they now knew to be a spaceship as well. The aliens did not go down—they were down, on the floor of the ocean, and anywhere else was up.

The alien Prime Minister nodded—a curiously human gesture. Dodge noticed for the first time as the thin arms were raised and the loose garment fell back the round shiny areas of skin, almost like scar-tissue, along the alien's ribs. Ferenc, noticing Dodge's interest, nudged him.

"Farewell." The Prime Minister appeared exhausted to Dodge's heightened, sympathetic perceptions. "I shall not see you again." He peered at them blindly.

Inside the submarine spaceship, Dodge felt an embarrassed humbleness, a catch in his throat, at the grave acceptance of the Prime Minister. The whole affair had the dreamy insubstantial quality of a drug-induced hallucination, and yet the strong bones of its moral structure forced a belief that he knew would outlast his present, almost maudlin sympathy. Even as he vowed to make events turn out right for the aliens as well as for humanity he wondered at himself; he had thought that the sparkling enthusiasms for romantic causes of youth had died in him long ago.

"Saw you looking at those scar-tissue discs," broke in Ferenc, the man of action, the dedicated, the understandable. "My guess is they are atrophied light organs. These folks probably used to light up splendidly before they developed."

"Like our cocyx, left over from tree-swinging," put in Harp. The harpooner had been oppressed, muted, by their recent experiences; now that they were turning back to the surface he emerged once again into command of himself

"Yes." Ferenc was obviously consumed by the fire of the discoveries they had been making. "But the most interesting thing was given me by our guide's contemptuous remark about our clumsy ultra-sonic equipment. Of course, these aliens see by ultra-sonics. Their eyes for visual light are all but useless. Did you notice the way they could stare right at a light without any significant pupil contraction? That lump over their forehead must contain ultra-sonic glands something like a bat's or a whale's."

Dodge, in his present wonderingly unsure frame of mind, pointed the obvious out for them. "All those lights," he said. "Put on for our benefit—"

"Impressive, at the least," Ferenc said. "Probably they do use light, though, for close work—"

"Decent of them, all the same," added Harp.

Dodge said: "They had to be given space travel. Radio

and Radar and TV would have been beyond them. They'd never have left their seas if they hadn't been given a helping hand." He did not add: "Who?" That would come later.

The journey back to the surface was occupied in careful decompression in the water-lock, the aliens working under the methodical directions of Pierre Ferenc. By the time the sub spaceship had altered course and risen alongside U.O.P. Base Trident, the three menfish were all but ready to leave. First, they relayed their information to Hardy, who at once contacted Dahlak Major, not without some triumph in his manner, and the jet-bomber was ordered back to base.

It was a quiet, simple, but disturbingly dramatic ending to interstellar war.

Dodge had been thinking a great deal about his own future. As they waited in the water-lock for final decompression and emergence into the six hundred feet deep U.O.P. Base, he was painfully aware of the whirling, frothy, inchoate mess of his thoughts and emotions. After what had happened to him, he supposed, he couldn't be expected to be able to laugh cheerily and dash off aboard a space cruiser for the next adventure. He wasn't built quite like that.

He and Harp had received the news that they could now undergo an operation, to enable them once again to breathe air, with mixed feelings. Dodge had been shocked at his own lack of enthusiasm.

"I must be getting water-logged in the brain," he told Ferenc as the aqua-valves opened. "I've got a funny feeling that I want to stay Under Ocean—actually that I want to live down here in this watery graveyard. Stupid, don't you think?"

"It's happened before," Ferenc said, too casually.

Their alien friend, busty in his pressure suit, saw them out with a grave courtesy. "One of my assistants went back to where we met," he said. "We felt guilty about parting you from your companion." A glinting speck moved under the alien lights, freeing itself from a towed cage.

"Huh?" said Ferenc.

Harp had understood, though, and he flashed a quick smile as Dodge ducked his head, rolled his arms and generally let Sally see that he was overjoyed to meet again. "Score aonther one for the aliens." He felt pleased, as though a conjecture had been proven true.

Inside the wet section of the base they were greeted by Simon Hardy, George Werner and Henderson all eagerly flying around, trying to say something before the previous speaker had finished. Dodge had little surprise that these important men were menfish, too. He'd expected it. He saw with envy the opercula over their gill slits giving them when in air an almost normal appearance. He'd have a pair of those, he'd been told. They were perfectly at home in air or water, these men, and like Ferenc, they impressed Dodge by the sheer vitality and rightness of their bodies; he knew that their brains and spirits were fully worthy of their superb vehicles. Captain Pinhorn, wearing a face-mask and breathing equipment and emitting pretty little fairychains of pearly bubbles, looked completely out of place. It was most disturbing. It was as though the menfish were members of an exclusive club, initiation into which demanded something special from a man that only the very cream of the world's best could ever hope to enter.

Commander Jeremy Dodge began to feel at home.

The two events that had overturned his life were connected, he could see that clearly, now. He could never have made contact with the aliens and brought his special Space Force attitude to bear if he hadn't been a manfish; and if a man without that spatial technique had not been on hand, the whole situation might have gone sour. He could almost call it fate, although he was much too hard-headed and too convinced of his own powers of making a stupid decision, to rely very much on fate. He had been taken below the surface of the sea and the aliens had fitted into his life as though waiting for him to arrive.

But, equally truthfully, if he had been a manfish only, and had never contacted the aliens, he would now be feeling something as he had felt when they'd found the farm destroyed and Elise and Lura gone. As though there was nothing much left for them. He and Harp would have been on their way back to Neptunia, on a mission they knew to be hopeless. The prospect of breathing air would have meant little, too—if they could ever have believed in it; he could admit that now with complete honesty.

Pinhorn was talking about space. Hardy was rumbling on, his stump jerking, about co-operation and build-up on the ocean floor. Dodge knew simply that he had finished with divided loyalties.

"Symbiosis. That's what it is!" Dodge burst out. Everyone swung around, flippers finning, to stare at him. Dodge laughed self-consciously. "You've told me that this Grosvenor fellow had Miss Tarrant and myself captured, along with Lura and her brother. So that's settled. But what I was thinking was that it it hadn't been for Danny Agostini taking us in that raid and being able to hide us because we were in my uncle's own farm—at least, mine now, I suppose—I'd never have been made over into a manfish. And, in that event . . ."

"I don't think I could have handled the aliens by myself," said Ferenc. "Those first few moments—they were very tricky."

"But the real thing is this," Dodge said with a passionate conviction that he knew, now, was quite sincere. "Simbiosis. Ocean and Space. One and One make the biggest number you can think of!" He let it all tumble out of him, anyhow. "Some men go back to the sea for food and powersources; they make a return journey to the womb. It's nice to keep the planet going on its own resources, it's good and rewarding and something desperately necessary. Why go to space? they ask. And the spacemen venture forth to the chips of light, knowing that one day a new race of men will arise out there in the vasty dark; and they tend to be contemptuous of the stick-at-home boys. They realize, but ignore the fact that their food must be provided from Earth, and that Earth has barely any surplus for fully dependent colonies on other worlds; unless the seas are worked to their utmost."

They were all gradually sinking to the floor now, to the functionally comfortable three-dimensional chairs, watching him with various expressions; but Dodge knew what he had to say was getting home—because these men already knew it and had refused to listen to themselves. Toxter ought to hear this—he would, too. Hardy would see to that.

"You can't conquer the stars until you've conquered the seas!" He flung out a hand, stopped, and then went on more quietly: "At least—you won't do it and maintain a civilized standard of life for those left on Earth."

Silence. A round port in the wall opened and a fat, chubby, cheerful fish swam in, its pot belly draped by a wicker framework, its opening and closing mouth like the silent essence of a choir. Hardy chuckled.

"Beautifully timed!" He snapped his fingers and the fish nuzzled his hand. "We all agree with you, Commander. But this time I think we can do something about these ideals. Space and Ocean! One and indivisible! A toast on it."

He began pulling flasks from the wicker cage on the corpulent fish's back, handing them round. Dodge put his cupped non-return valved spout into his mouth.

Hardly chuckled. "This isn't water, gentlemen. Just this once."

Henderson said: "Space—and Ocean."

They all drank deep.

Lieutenant Benedek, his conical helmet with slats open tucked smartly under his arm, came in and reported to Hardy. Hardy looked over at Dodge and a smile wrinkled his eyes.

"Well, tell him, then, Benedek. You nearly spotted him once before, remember?"

Lieutenant Benedek flew across to Dodge and said: "Admiral's compliments, sir. A Miss Tarrant would like to see . . ."

Dodge was finning through the doorway before the lieutenant had finished. Someone in the room chuckled. Harp, with the single name: "Lura!" on his lips, scissored from the floor, finned after Dodge. Benedek adjusted his conical casque, saluted, and followed.

The room was small and square with a light fixture in the center of the ceiling. One wall was a sheet of transparent plastic. Through it the other half of the room was just as bare, glaring in its single light, but there was a chair positioned close to the transparent wall.

On Dodge's side he breathed water. On the other side— he would have drowned in air.

She rose from the chair and came towards the glass wall,

hands outstretched. The two-way communicator carried her voice clearly. Dodge pressed against the glass.

"Jerry—that is—I'm glad you're safe . . ."

"Elise—that Agostini . . ."

She smiled awkwardly with remembrance of unpleasantness.

"I'm afraid Lura was rough with him." Her eyes met his with perfect candor. "We helped to put him in the sub-tow balloon. Lura wanted to leave him to those terrible barracuda; but I suggested he'd look better in a court."

Sally flicked around his head. He smiled gratefully.

"Elise," he said gravely. "I'd like you to meet Sally." He pushed water at the dazzling pilot fish. "Sally—this is Elise." It sounded inadequate.

He could see her face; after one sweeping glance which took in those three scraps of defiant scarlet, he could see only her face. So like the last time—and yet now there was all the world before him, if . . .

"Elise," he said slowly, uncertainly. "I shall be having the operation very soon; I'll be able to breathe air again." He gulped, and spat as he tasted sea-water for the first time unpleasantly. He'd become so used to it, and yet now, just talking about breathing air again, he was rebelling.

"Sorry. Quite getting to feeling at home undersea. Elise —when I'm a normal man again, will you . . ."

She stopped him. "Jerry. One thing. I know how you must have felt when you were first press-ganged. I've lost sleep night after night thinking about it. I've been in mental agony—and yet I'm not pleading." She closed her eyes and said firmly: "Jerry—I arranged for you to be kidnapped. Lura and her brother were to help." She opened her eyes and rushed on: "But Grosvenor tricked me. All I wanted to do was to let you see something of what went on on the farms. I thought—you were a spaceman hero— you'd have no time even to go undersea. You'd just take the profits and be off back to your stupid little balls of mud up in the sky." Her voice broke.

Dodge said gently: "All right, Elise. It's all right. I supposed I must have guessed. And Grosvenor had us all kidnapped? So he could take over?"

"I don't know. I don't think so. When he rang up your hotel I guessed something was going to happen, I was frightened that my plans had been discovered; yet I had to go on. I thought that if you saw the undersea farm's conditions, then you'd do something to stop the cruelty. Grosvenor found out. He saw his fat profits going—or, maybe, he really did want to take over. He stayed undersea all the time—he had surgery, like yours, only supposed to be perfect; but it didn't turn out right. He's a little bitter."

"Under Ocean are the only people legally allowed to perform this operation, on volunteers," Dodge said. "Sure, I feel sorry for the guy; but he was playing with fire and got burnt." His voice changed. "But that doesn't matter, now. When I've finished this op, and get out, will you . . ."

"I'll race you," said Elise.

"Huh?"

"I'll beat you to it."

"To what?" Dodge put his face against the glass and peered hard, his nose flattened and bloodless. "Oh, no! You mean you're going to become a mermaid?"

"Too right."

The door opened and a comfortable matronly woman walked in. She smiled and signalled to Elise.

Elise turned to the transparent wall again.

"I used my womanly wiles on the surgeon so they'd operate on me first. I'll be a mermaid whilst you're still out on the table. Clever, aren't I?"

"You just wait . . ."

"Why—I shouldn't think any girl would want a husband who could slink off under the sea when he felt like it. No telling what tricks you'd get up to down there."

"You just wait until I can lay a hand on you," growled Dodge. He pushed his mouth forward. Sally, glittering, tumbled around delightedly. Elise, on the other side of the glass, pressed her lips against the outline of Dodge's; one in air, the other in water, they kissed.

Dodge could have sworn the water on his side heated up.

SCIENCE FICTION AND FANTASY
FROM AVON ◆ BOOKS

INTIMACY . . .
BEYOND ECSTASY . . .
BEYOND TIME . . .

MINDBRIDGE

BY NEBULA AND HUGO AWARD WINNER

JOE HALDEMAN

**"FANTASTIC . . . A MINDBLITZ
. . . BRINGS OUT ALL THE TERROR WE REPRESS AT
THE POSSIBILITY OF HOW EASILY WE MIGHT BE
POSSESSED BY A STRONGER POWER."**
Los Angeles Times

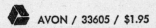 AVON / 33605 / $1.95

MIND 7-79

THE BEST IN SCIENCE FICTION AND FANTASY FROM AVON ⬡ BOOKS

URSULA K. LE GUIN

The Lathe of Heaven	43547	1.95
The Dispossessed	44057	2.25

ISAAC ASIMOV

Foundation	44057	1.95
Foundation and Empire	42689	1.95
Second Foundation	45351	1.95
The Foundation Trilogy (Large Format)	26930	4.95

ROGER ZELAZNY

Doorways in the Sand	49510	1.75
Creatures of Light and Darkness	35956	1.50
Lord of Light	44834	2.25
The Doors of His Face The Lamps of His Mouth	38182	1.50
The Guns of Avalon	31112	1.50
Nine Princes in Amber	36756	1.50
Sign of the Unicorn	30973	1.50
The Hand of Oberon	33324	1.50
The Courts of Chaos	47175	1.75

Include 50¢ per copy for postage and handling,
allow 4-6 weeks for delivery.

Avon Books, Mail Order Dept.
224 W. 57th St., N.Y., N.Y. 10019